Marguerite Dickens

Along Shore with a Man-of-war

Marguerite Dickens

Along Shore with a Man-of-war

ISBN/EAN: 9783337009267

Printed in Europe, USA, Canada, Australia, Japan

Cover: Foto ©Andreas Hilbeck / pixelio.de

More available books at **www.hansebooks.com**

ALONG SHORE

WITH A MAN-OF-WAR

BY

MARGUERITE DICKINS

BOSTON, MASS.:

Arena Publishing Company,

COPLEY SQUARE,

1893.

INTRODUCTION.

WHEN I first joined the United States Navy, by means of a marriage certificate, I found that a properly equipped sailor carried the Spanish language in his mental kit, so I acquired it and have enjoyed the possession immensely, especially when taking the journey of which this book gives all the details that I thought would please the public.

For two years and a half I sailed up and down the east coast of South America; seeing the lovely scenery; meeting the officials, and private families; talking to and visiting them; reading the books they loaned me, or I could buy, until I felt quite at home among them and made many friends.

My letters home were so much enjoyed, and so many have praised those of them that were published in the press, that I venture to test the value and sincerity of their words by launching these letters in a volume, trusting they may help to pleasantly wile away some hours for some one.

MARGUERITE DICKINS.

TABLE OF CONTENTS.

CHAPTER   PAGE

     I. MOUTH OF THE AMAZON 7
    II. CITY OF MARANHAM 14
   III. CITY OF PERNAMBUCO 19
   IV. CITY OF BAHIA 24
    V. RIO DE JANEIRO 30
   VI. RIO DE JANEIRO 40
  VII. RIO DE JANEIRO 48
 VIII. THE RIO DE LA PLATA—MONTEVIDEO . . . 59
   IX. SCENES IN MONTEVIDEO 67
    X. OSTRICHES IN URUGUAY—VISIT TO SENOR SAPELLO'S BIRD FARM NEAR PIEDRAS . . . 77
   XI. CLOSING CEREMONIES OF A CONGRESS OF SOUTHERN REPUBLICS 85
  XII. HOTELS IN MONTEVIDEO—THE FAVORITE BATHING RESORTS 93
 XIII. THE CARNIVAL SEASON IN THE GAY CAPITAL OF URUGUAY 100
 XIV. A BULL-FIGHT IN MONTEVIDEO 107
  XV. CITY OF BUENOS AYRES 117
 XVI. SHOPS OF BUENOS AYRES 124
 XVII. OBJECTS OF INTEREST IN THE SUBURBS OF BUENOS AYRES 131
XVIII. THE CITY OF LA PLATA 138
 XIX. UP THE URUGUAY RIVER—CITY OF COLONIA . . 145
  XX. PAYSANDU AND THE CAPITAL OF ENTRE RIOS . . 158
 XXI. UP THE RIVER URUGUAY—NUEVA PALMYRA . . 163
 XXII. FRAY BENTOS 169
XXIII. AFLOAT ON THE PARANA 175
XXIV. UP THE GREAT RIVER TO THE MODERN CITY OF ROSARIO 182
 XXV. A TRIP TO CORDOBA 189
XXVI. FROM ROSARIO TO SANTA ELENA AND CITIES BY THE WAY 206
XXVII. LA PAZ TO CORRIENTES 213
XXVIII. THE CITY OF ASUNCION—ELEVEN HUNDRED MILES UP THE PARANA AND PARAGUAY . . 219
XXIX. THE PLACE OF LOPEZ 225
 XXX. THE ANNIVERSARY OF THE INDEPENDENCE OF PARAGUAY 232
XXXI. SUBURBS OF ASUNCION 237

LIST OF ILLUSTRATIONS.

PORTRAIT OF AUTHOR.

U.S.S. TALLAPOOSA, MONTEVIDEO HARBOR.

GROUP OF PALMS, BRAZIL.

RIO DE JANEIRO, BRAZIL.

AVENUE OF PALMS, BOTANICAL GARDEN, RIO DE JANEIRO.

TIJUCA, BRAZIL.

MONTEVIDEO, FROM THE CERRO.

INDEPENDENCE SQUARE, MONTEVIDEO.

VICTORIA SQUARE, BUENOS AYRES.

GROUP OF AMERICANS, CORDOBA, ARGENTINE.

HANDKERCHIEF PARAGUAYAN LACE.

ALONG SHORE WITH A MAN-OF-WAR.

I.

MOUTH OF THE AMAZON.

SCENES IN THE CITY OF PARA—TROY-MADE CARS ON THE
STREET RAILROADS—THE HOTELS AND MARKETS—A VISIT
TO " MONKEY JOE'S "—THE CLIMATE AND PEOPLE.

A LONG stretch of sandy beach to the south, masses of tum-
bled, dirty water to the north, and a narrow winding channel
beneath our keel; this was the mouth of the mighty Amazon.
And things did not improve much as we made our way up.
The sky line of Marajo Island is a dead level; a distant line of
tropical forest, unbroken and uninteresting, except as one
peoples it with animals, savages, birds, flowers or anything else
that fancy suggests, according as one's imagination is inclined
to the beautiful or the savage. The right bank we gradually

approached, and here and there was a clearing, with a red-roofed house, or perhaps there was a glimpse of the roofs of a tiny village, all the roofs of the same bright red tiles, which were evidently made in the many brick-yards that nestled close down to the water against the bank or perched on some tiny bluff.

The tiles that they make are like the old curved Dutch ones, and are used exclusively for roofs. The bricks are shaped like a small carpenter's square when viewed end on, and have three square openings clear through them ; they are also longer and broader than our bricks. As we approached Para there were islands near us which narrowed the channel until we seemed really to be in a river. Still, the islands and banks were not attractive—always low and monotonous, the dense growth of trees reaching down to and often dipping into the water, the masses of vines running over and drooping from them. The occasional bits of slimy bank all looked gloomy, forbidding, and miasmatic, in spite of the blending of the beautiful shades of green in the different plants.

About 6:30 our anchor dropped, and we swung into our berth off the City of Para, but had hardly more than a glimpse of her shining buildings before the sun set, and in three minutes it was dark, the stars above, twinkling lamplights in the city, and numerous bonfires alone lighting up in a vague way the city. It was a feast day, hence the bonfires before the churches, the band of music playing loudly, and the rockets which went up from all parts of the place. The next day we went ashore early, and landed at a nice covered wharf—a wharf is a luxury any one who has traveled much appreciates, and a covered one is more than luxury.

First we found a long, narrow park fronting the river, planted with palm trees, and around the base of one was a group of half-naked, brown-skinned boys, gambling with their copper pennies, and they were much amused when I resented their calling me English; but I know by experience that to the South American, to be a citizen of the United States is to be a friend, and to be English is the contrary. Behind the park, facing the river, is a row of large two-storied buildings, their fronts entirely covered with glazed tiles. The effect was beautiful as they shone and sparkled in the tropical sun, and as most of the buildings and residences in the city were entirely covered with these tiles, brought from Portugal, you can fancy what a gay city it is. The bank building, where we changed some money, was covered with pale green tiles, a pink conventional rose in relief being in the center of each one. Apropos of money, for an English sovereign we received 11,000 paper reis, a rei being the unit of value used in Brazil. The smallest copper coin used is a piece of twenty reis—one cent— and what one uses most commonly are the one and two hundred nickel reis pieces, and the one, two, five, and ten mil—thousand—reis bank notes. Their paper money, like that of most of the world, is made by the American Bank Note Company of New York, and is very pretty when new.

We went to the market, walking along one of the many paved streets with stone sidewalks, and found it in a large white-washed building which had a court or patio in the center. A patio is a closed or open court, with or without flowers in it, and often forming the chief feature in a house. There were piles of fruit all about on the stands; among them, bananas of many varieties, pine-apples, avocates, sapodillas, cocoa-nuts, oranges, limes, and many others that were new to me. Two stands had decorated gourds; there were a few chattering monkeys, screaming parrots, and smaller birds. There were a few Brazil nuts, both in and out of the husk, but it was not the season for them, and I here learned that the sole source of the world's supply was the Upper Amazon. The natives, who bring them down in big canoes, are often a month on the voyage down and two or three on the return, if they ever return, for they often break up their canoes and remain in Para, appalled by the difficulties of the return trip against the swift river.

The street cars are like the open ones we use in summer, and were made by John Stephenson, of Troy, N. Y. They are drawn by two fair-sized rats with long ears, which are called mules to flatter them. They go at a gallop most of the time, and as the tracks are much neglected and in a state to give you sudden surprises, you wish you had the driving to do. Some one must have had *carte-blanche* given him to put down street-car tracks, for they are on all of the principal, all of the side streets, and most of the alleys, besides running well out into the country. Most of the streets are shaded by mango trees. This tree has a large trunk with a smooth bark; the foliage is bright green and very dense; the fruit about the size of a goose egg, smooth, bright yellow, the pulp clinging firmly to the pit; it is also sweet and tastes strongly of turpentine. There is a stretch of palms down one street that they seemed very proud of, and they were beautiful; but palms are indigenous, and if they like them so much, why not have a lot? The tiled houses, situated behind gardens full of blooming plants, looked lovely, and the wild, luxuriant growths in the suburbs were fascinating; but we could not linger long, as the thermometer stood at about 120°, and every one but myself complained of the heat.

We went to the principal hotel and had a poor dinner, with good native wine, in a nice, cool, clean room, with blooming plants on the balconies, through which we looked at the crowded streets below. Water is taken to the houses in big barrels mounted on wheels and drawn by the tiniest oxen and bulls; they are hardly larger than a calf. The men's dress, among the lower class, is a cotton shirt and trousers; the women's dress is more gay and decidedly picturesque; long trailing gowns of bright-hued cotton goods cut low-neck and without sleeves, their hair combed back over a high cushion, and this exaggerated pompadour puff ornamented with any number of natural flowers, put in apparently as we stick pins in a pin-cushion.

After dinner we started for "Monkey Joe's," his commercial name, and on the way passed many commission houses that deal in rubber, nuts, chocolate, beans, and so on. The rubber is in large, round, dark-colored lumps, and most of it well mixed with sand and small sticks. It is sewed up in burlaps and tin-tags put on to mark it; when one of these bundles drops into the hold of a ship it bounds up again as if it were alive. "Monkey Joe" had no fine onca skins, but promised to get one soon for one of our party. The onca is the native leopard of South America, and grows to an immense size. The markings are beautiful, and the natives generally call them tigers. Joe's stock of live animals was low; he had only a sloth, an electric eel, and a splendid boa-constrictor. The latter was wandering around at will, and when a drunken native took hold of its head and began hitting it on the floor to wake it up we left, but not before we had seen the Sapucaia nut, which grows in a bowl-shaped pod, with a cover that can be taken off and put on again. The inside bark of the tree is used to make coarse brooms for sweeping streets and such purposes. We also secured some beetles and tonka-beans.

Para is a growing, busy place, and is bound to be a great emporium, as it is a distributing point for an immense interior. The climate is deadly—as bad as that of the Isthmus—and besides fevers, there is a disease called beri-beri, which does not seem to be very well understood. A lady who was dying of it told me it was like creeping paralysis. Para is a name given to the city by traders, and it has now been accepted by the government, but the original name was Belem—Bethlehem.

II.

CITY OF MARANHAM.

A QUAINT OLD CITY THAT HAS SEEN ITS BEST DAYS—THE
STREETS AND PLAZAS—THE BISHOP'S COMFORTABLE PAL-
ACE AND CHARMING GARDEN—OTHER PLACES OF IN-
TEREST.

OFTEN when picking their way over piles of rubbish and
building materials that so frequently encumber our streets, I
have heard people wish that they could once find a town
that was finished. They ought to visit Maranham, which
was our next port after Para. Maranham is finished, and is
rapidly decaying; the city was once large and thriving, its port
filled with vessels of many nations; but the climate and beri-beri
have done their work; the harbor is almost deserted, and
a melancholy air of decay and mold pervades the place. The
channel is winding, and as the pilot wished to give himself all
the chances, he waited until high tide, which came at nine
o'clock in the evening.

Then, in the bright moonlight, he took us in, gradually
approaching a half-ruined old fort which was built by the

Dutch when they held this part of the coast. The fort is built on an island, and behind it was a lovely landlocked bay, the lights of the city gleaming in tiers on the farther side, as the streets of the city wandered here and there on the steep hill side. Early next morning we were on deck, ready to go on shore, but we had to wait a few minutes for a tropical shower to pass over. It poured down as if all the flood-gates were opened, for a few minutes, then the heavy clouds moved on, the sun came out, the boatman pulled the cover off his boat, and, stepping in, we were rapidly pulled ashore.

We landed at a low, old, stone water battery, with a few miserable cannon mounted here and there, en barbette, upon it. From here we walked up a very steep street, and found ourselves in a long, rather narrow plaza, with four rows of palm trees and some scanty grass growing in it. On the side next the bay was a long, two-storied yellow building called the palace. Every door and window stood open, and here and there were officers or soldiers loafing on the balconies and at the main entrance, smoking cigarettes. There were some nice houses on the other side of the plaza, covered with glazed tiles ; their gardens full of flowers, with fountains and seats, the latter made of adobe and also covered with glazed tiles. In front of the palace we took a street-car, drawn by two tiny mules scarcely larger than those at Para, and they took us through narrow streets, keeping pretty well on the ridge of the hill next the bay until we reached the Plaza Remedios.

This plaza is a large, long terrace, commanding a very beautiful view of the harbor, with its shipping, city, and outer bay. It is rather ill-kept, but there were a good many fine palm trees and a fairly good statue of Goncalves Diaz, the poet. Behind the plaza was the large stucco palace of the bishop, and as we could catch a glimpse of a lovely garden through a gate, we rang the bell and asked if we could see it. Antonio Cudido da Almerenga, bishop of Maranham, was not at home, having gone on a trip into the interior for the benefit of his health; but the young man in charge, who seemed to be all alone in the immense building, said he would show us about with pleasure.

The palace is built along two sides of a square, the other two sides being enclosed by a brick wall, thus hiding the lovely garden from the world, except as you get a glimpse through the gate. The building is a story and a half in height or one story with a high basement, and you enter by a long flight of steps through big double doors. The hall is a wide, generous one, and runs clear around the building, one side being entirely of glass to give an uninterrupted view of the garden; the other side has numerous doors which lead into different rooms. We were shown a reception room and a parlor, the furniture in each being arranged in the Spanish style; that is, a sofa placed against the wall, extending from the sofa out towards the center of the room, two rows of chairs, facing each other, and in the center of the room a table. In the parlor there were two arrangements of this kind. The sofa is the seat of honor, and here the most distinguished guest sits with the host or hostess. There were plenty of embroidered cushions on the sofas, and over one hung a picture of the bishop in his robes. He had a fine, pleasing, Spanish face.

The chapel was neat, small and in good order; the altar having nothing worthy of note upon it. The dining-room was large and cheerful, with a large stone terrace outside the windows, and from this terrace one overlooked the Plaza Remedios and the lovely view beyond. The garden was divided into two parts by a terrace, the upper part being filled with fruit trees, while the lower was a mass of bloom— hibiscus, four-o'clocks, cypress vine, tea roses, and chrysanthemums hobnobbishly, with the numerous tropical flowers, making the place a delight. The cistern and bath-house were of glazed tiles and the latter looked so cool and refreshing that one longed for a dip in the large sunken tub.

We took a car back to the street nearest the market and then got out and walked down the very narrow, steep thing called a street. Luckily it was not wider or it would have held more dirt. We stepped into a little shop and bought some pretty colored calabashes of a queer little old man, and in the market

2

I was tempted to buy a cunning little ring-tailed monkey, but finally compromised by filling his paws full of bananas, and he even took one in his tail and longed to grab more, but five were all he could hold. There was very little fruit on the stands and nothing else at that time of the day, so we left and wandered around the streets, which were generally narrow and very dirty in spite of the frequent rains.

The shops were poor, and to judge by the houses, there is very little wealth. We stopped at a cabinetmaker's to see a pet onca kitten and found him and his men making very pretty furniture of a native red cedar, the odor of which was delicious. The tools used were of the clumsiest description. Two men were sawing a log into boards with a saw that looked as if it were made in the time of Noah. There was nothing peculiar about the dress of the people, except the prevalence of patchwork calico jackets among the men.

III.

CITY OF PERNAMBUCO.

AN ISLAND WHOSE INHABITANTS ARE CONVICTS—FUNERAL CUSTOMS—SUGAR WAREHOUSES—A BRAZILIAN POETESS— THE CUSTOM OF KISSING AMONG THE WOMEN.

RECIFE, or Pernambuco, as it is now called, looks like a bit of Holland from outside the harbor. There are the tall houses with the steep roofs, several stories in height, with big gable ends, and finally the narrow streets, looking like mere cracks. It is built along a rather straight stretch of shore, and it would be impossible to have a city there were it not for nature's help, in the shape of a high steep-to recife, or reef of rock, which extends along in front of the city, and, making a perfect breakwater, leaves a long, narrow, safe harbor. It is rather narrow for all the shipping, so each vessel has to moor, but it is large enough, and a wonderful bit of natural work. The part of the town next the harbor was all built by the Dutch, and the streets are so very narrow that there is not room for two wagons to pass. There are street-car lines on nearly all of them, and as the streets twist and turn in all directions you are soon deafened by the noise, bewildered as to direction, and disagreeably hustled by passers-by. There is a broad river, which winds about through the city, and this gives a chance for many pretty effects, and in the new, or Brazilian part of the city, they are utilized. Many fine bridges span the stream, and gardens run down to it, the palace garden being especially pretty in this respect.

We were invited to spend the day at the home of a missionary in the suburbs, and were very glad to shut ourselves up in their pretty garden, eat sapodillas, talk of Brazil, and forget all about the ship. It was a long ride in the street-cars, and we obtained a good idea of the city. There was a fine-looking opera-house, and just beyond it, while crossing a bridge, we saw a flat-boat filled with convicts bound for the convict island of San Juan de Naronha, which lies a short distance off the coast. They were ordinary looking, dark-skinned natives, and sat quietly in their seats. After reading all the histories of South American countries I can find, and spending four years on the continent, it seems to me that the native Indian, has a good deal of belief in Kismet. After a certain amount of resistance he sits down, shrugs his shoulders, and submits to any amount of what seems intolerable cruelty. These men made me think of a herd of sheep, surrounded by vigilant, armed guards, who sat upon the edges of the boat. I was told that during the empire a man would not be given a life sentence, but was ordered to San Juan to await the pleasure of the emperor, and then the emperor would forget him.

Next we saw a hearse going to a child's funeral. It was white, wheels and all; was very tall, and seemed shaky and unsteady as it rattled over the poor pavements. The coachman was dressed in scarlet, and the windows of the hearse were draped with thin curtains of the same hue. Another funeral which we saw was that of a much-esteemed professor, and he, contrary to custom, was being carried to church by some of his friends and followed by a long line of mourners on foot. These mourners were all men, as it does not seem to be customary in this country for women to attend funerals, or to go anywhere else, for that matter ; but I will speak of this again.

The streets in the new city are broad, and there were many pretty houses in the suburbs, surrounded by gardens filled with flowers and shaded by palm and bread-fruit trees. The latter are very tall, with glossy, large, dark-green leaves that have a great many points and fruit that look like enormous button-balls showing here and there. I mean by button-balls the seed of the sycamore tree. The flower-gardens in South America are not at all like ours. When a house is built, all the grounds about it are dug up and divided off into beds, in which beds are planted the trees and flowers. Sometimes there are tiny boxwood hedges around each bed, but generally not. The space between them is graveled or paved for walks, and then the grounds are complete, unless a fountain or statues are added. It is the rarest thing that a blade of grass is allowed to grow, and I have only seen one house that had what we would call a lawn. Oxen are used a great deal to draw the long, narrow carts through the streets, and the merchants must be a patient lot if they are satisfied to await the delivery of their goods. The natives of the province make very pretty pillow-lace that looks something like torchon, and they do exquisite drawn work.

Pernambuco is a great port for the shipment of sugar, and there were rows of storehouses for its reception while awaiting shipment, and the odor of them was exceedingly disagreeable. We got some pine-apples here that are famous along the coast, and they were very sweet, but not better than those of Toboga Island near Panama.

When the final emancipation of the slaves was being agitated the province of Pernambuco vied with that of Rio Grande do Sul in being the most outspoken in favor of freedom. Many people of the province voluntarily emancipated those they held in bondage, and one wealthy man freed so many that he was ennobled by Isabella when she was Princess Imperial and Regent. I wanted to see a slave market, but they had been abolished before we reached the country.

On the steamer between Pernambuco and Bahia we made the acquaintance of a Brazilian poetess. She was short, plump, vivacious, and, like all the women of her nation, exceedingly fond of kissing. Every morning she would rush up and embrace me, kissing each cheek in turn, and then apologize by saying: "You know I am a Brazilian." She had a nice little girl, but oh, she was so frail and delicate, I fear she has gone aloft before now, yet hope not, for she was her mother's idol. The husband did not count for much, a neutral, colorless man. This custom of kissing every woman I met did not recommend itself to me, yet it was necessary to not only accept but practice it. However, I drew the line at dress-makers and lace women, although one lace woman got ahead of me by the suddenness of her attack.

IV.

CITY OF BAHIA.

ARRIVAL AT RIO JANEIRO, WHICH HAS THE MOST BEAUTIFUL
HARBOR IN THE WORLD—A PICTURESQUE BACKGROUND
OF MOUNTAINS—SCENES AT THE CUSTOM HOUSE.

OUR next port was San Salvador en Bahia de todos los
Santos, or Bahia Bay, as it is generally called. It is built
on one side of a beautiful bay, with lovely islands in it, and
consists of the lower and upper town. The lower is very
long and narrow, nestling between the bay and a steep cliff;
it consists of three or four streets, used principally, with the
exception of the market, by large merchants who have their
storehouses there. The main part of the city is built on top
of the bluff, and extends way out into the country. We went
ashore as early as possible so as to see the market, and when
we first landed we seemed to have stepped into fairyland.
Great African negresses, some of them with tatooed faces,
sat guarding piles of luscious fruit, their large forms draped
in white cotton gowns cut low in the neck. They all wore
necklaces, bracelets, and ear-rings, and here and there was a
turban. Lounging about were their mates, who are much val-

ued as porters. They are all of pure African blood, and keep
to themselves, disdaining alliance with any other race. The
oranges these woman sold us are the finest in the world; you
eat none like them anywhere else. They will average a
pound in weight; the rind is soft and brittle, which prevents
their transportation—the juice is very sweet and high-flavored;
they are also seedless. They are the navel orange, and those
of Florida are a poor offspring of plants from Bahia; it needs
its climate, soil, and sunny slopes to produce the perfect
fruit. There were piles of lemons, limes, pine-apples, sapodillas, bananas; vegetables of many kinds; coops of chickens
and doves; stalls of native pottery, red, with white ornamenta-
tion; piles of cages with small birds; rows of parrots, cocka-
toos, big blue and red macaws; numberless monkeys, from the
tiny little marmosets to big ring-tails—prehensile tails; quantities of wicker-work; kiosks where coffee, and a number
of drinks made from different fruits were sold; in short,
a tropical market.

We stayed there some time and then took an elevator at the
base of the bluff and were hoisted by steam to the top. Here
we found the usual Brazilian city, and we rode all about it,
finally alighting at the public gardens, which have been beautiful, but now are much neglected. There were some beautiful
mango and palm trees and what had been a fine lot of flower
beds, but the ants had gotten at them and not much remained.

There was a rather plain monument to the regent John, and the remains of a large tiled terrace just on the edge of the bluff, with broken statues and tiled seats. From here we had a lovely view of the curving bay, with its green shores, blue waters, and many vessels riding quietly at anchor, the whole scene illuminated by the brilliant sun. Next the terrace was the fort of St. George. We heard drums rolling, and a brilliant looking officer on a white horse came out and rode away. We visited a diamond merchant and saw some beautiful gems from the adjacent mines, cut and uncut. This is also a great city for the manufacture of feather-flowers; they are carefully made and are beautiful, because the birds of Brazil furnish feathers of all colors and shades, as nature can be copied very closely in unfading tints. Bundles are carried on the head, regardless of the size. One sees a woman stalking along with a tiny bundle poised on high, another with a large basket of oranges, carrying it with apparently the same ease; but when six men get a piano on their heads they move slowly, and are careful to keep step.

Early one morning we were awakened by a loud knocking at the stateroom door, and a voice announced that the captain sent his compliments, and we were to come up on the bridge as soon as possible, for we were very near Rio. It was pitch dark, but we scrambled into our clothes and reached the pilot-house just as the day was breaking. To our left we

U. S. S. TALLAPOOSA, MONTEVIDEO HARBOR.

could see a low island with a light-house on it, the light
burning brightly, and to the right the islands of Mai and Pai,
while in front of us rose ranges of high towering mountains,
seemingly an impenetrable mass. However, as the day grew
brighter, we saw a broad, clean-cut opening in the nearest
chain, and this was the entrance to the most beautiful harbor
in the world. The mountains to the left of the entrance
gradually assumed the form of a giant lying on his back,
the face and feet being especially plain. Gradually the sun
began to appear, and then we were near enough to see the
beautiful, waving palms standing out from the masses of
brilliant green foliage that covered each and every mountain
from its base to its summit. Here and there a white house
caught the light and shone like a gem. In the distance
were ranges of mountains, some gray where they lay in the
shadow, some pink where the sun had reached them, varied
in shape, graceful in outline, covered with magnificent
growths. The mountains about Rio stand unequaled, unsur-
passed. The water was blue as a sapphire, and as we plowed
our way through it up the bay, we first saw a fort, then, on the
opposite side of the bay, Botofoga, with its white and yellow
houses clustered about it, and from there, for miles stretching
along at the foot of the mountains, following each bend of the
slope, built over the foothills, and even extending up on to the
nearest mountains, was the beautiful city of Rio de Janeiro,

or Saint Sebastian, as it was formerly called. The beautiful blue waters, the curves and bends of the shore, followed by the beautiful city, the low hills covered with gleaming white houses, churches, and gardens, the background of beautiful mountains that stretch north, south, and west and sweep around the bay, and the blue sky over all, made a picture that, once seen, you could never forget.

Did you ever cherish a dream for years and suddenly wake to find it realized? Well, I had dreamed of the tropics and eagerly read all I could find about them, until my mind was filled with dreams of waving palms, luxuriant strange growths, forests where every tree was strange, where creepers twined and twisted about, and the great brilliant orchid flowers vied with the butterflies. Then I went to the tropics, and disappointment met me on every side, even on the Isthmus of Panama, and I felt my dream was but a dream, never to be realized. When, lo! I enter the harbor of Rio, and all I asked and more lies before me, and one can never be disappointed, disenchanted, for at the end of the dirtiest, narrowest street there is always a vista of lovely mountains that is fine enough to lift you above the dirt and bad odors. However, the city is an unusually clean one, and the narrow streets are not by any means as numerous as the wide ones. We steamed past the man-of-war anchorage and slowed down off the custom-house, while the immense mail we carried was

dropped over the side, and then we proceeded on our way up
to our own anchorage off the old part of the city. A launch
was sent for us, and taking a boat in tow, which held our
baggage, we were soon at the custom-house wharf, and were
welcomed by the officials with bows, and handed chairs to
occupy until the trunks arrived. The first thing I noticed was
the number of men going about with their jaws tied up and
plaid shawls over their shoulders. I afterwards saw a great
many in the same rig, but never could find out what was the
matter with them. They were as grave, solemn, and polite
as the other people, yet you had to control your desire to
smile audibly as one after another struck your eye. When the
trunks came we were requested, with many bows, to be good
enough to unlock them, and here we began to practice the
system of bowing that is prevalent all over this continent. No
matter what trouble you put a person to if you smile and bow,
and say, thank you, just before leaving, they count all their
trouble as nothing. We were bowed to and thanked for
unlocking the trunks. Each tray was lifted out and imme-
diately put back and the trunks locked. There were many
apologies for the trouble they had given us, and we were
profuse with our assertions that we had not been inconven-
ienced. Everybody bowed and bowed, and we walked out with
a gentleman from the steamship company who had been sent
to see us safe at our hotel.

V.

RIO DE JANEIRO.

THE SUBURBS OF THE CAPITAL—BY CABLE ROAD TO THE
RESERVOIRS THAT SUPPLY THE CITY—COMFORTS OF A
BRAZILIAN HOTEL—ASCENT OF THE CORCOVADO—WON-
DERFUL LAND AND SEA VIEWS.

THERE is one especially beautiful walk in the suburbs of Rio
de Janeiro, which is known as Santa Teresa, and we were soon
introduced to it by our friends. Leaving a street-car, or *bonde*,
as they are called there, in a narrow street, one enters quite a
good-sized station, placed at the foot of one of the mountains,
and finds a cable-car waiting. The platform inclines steeply,
while one end of the car is much lower than the other. The
track seems to go straight up a precipice, and is built on a
jutting ledge or spur, the cable being worked from the top.
The track is about 1,000 yards long, and as the car went up
there were lovely views of the city, bay, and mountains to
enjoy.

Nictherog, a small city across the bay, looked especially
pretty, all its houses white in the dazzling sunshine. Steep

banks came close up to the track on either side, but they were not too steep to be clothed with shrubs and trees, and the coffee trees had berries which then were bright and red, all ready to eat; the pulp around the seeds tasting slightly sweet and not unpleasant, but still a long way from our cherries that they are likened to.

Arriving at the end of the railway, we take a *bonde*, drawn by four mules, which stands waiting, and is dragged still further up, but here the road is laid out on a sort of natural terrace, with houses and villas on either side, some of them boasting lovely gardens, and all commanding a superb view of part of the city, the upper part of the bay, ranges of lofty mountains, and beautiful valleys over which clouds are always floating, casting wonderful shadows. One rich valley lies just beneath them, and one would fancy the happy dwellers on these heights would spend all their lives gazing on the perfect scene with never-ending delight. The mules dash through a little town and come to a halt at the beginning of a broad forest road, so well kept that it is daily swept with brooms in addition to other attentions.

A few steps away is the lower reservoir for supplying the city, which is surrounded by a pretty little garden full of flowers. Benches are placed where they command the grand view, and in one corner is a nice little house for the attendants. There are five tanks, but one is emptied each day to

clean it out, so only four were filled with water, which was
so clear, bright, and sparkling that one doubly enjoyed
drinking it while in the city after visiting the reservoir.
On the left of the broad road is the aqueduct, built by the
Jesuits in 1746, and it is still the source of water supply
for the city, trying as best it can to keep pace with the
growing burg, in which it succeeds pretty well. It is built
of adobe as strong as stone, and is generally about five feet
high. Two cemented ducts are on the bottom of the inside,
one always in use, and the other kept ready in case of an
accident. The roof is ridge-shaped, with dormers facing the
road. Every few feet, in the front of each of these dormers,
is a small iron grating, and by. putting one's ear close to
any one of them the water can be heard running along inside.

The road follows the aqueduct and the ridge of the
mountain until it melts into another grander mountain. It
lies in the forest its entire length; coffee and numberless
other lovely shrubs growing in greatest profusion on either
side, while closer to the earth were delicate ferns and pretty,
strange, wild flowers; the whole shaded by tall palms and
trees that had nothing familiar about them, some even having three-cornered trunks. The trunks and branches—enough
of the latter reaching out to arch in the road—were dotted
every here and there with orchids, plants that flourish here
on the rich moist air and have strange bright blossoms.

From tree branch to tree branch hung hundreds of vines, some of them large, some small, but all lithe and graceful, with every here and there the trunk of a tree half smothered in their embrace.

One can pass hours in this enchanting forest, gazing here and there, always discovering some new tree, plant, or other growth that had hitherto escaped notice ; and as one passes along the road where it winds slowly up the other mountain, glimpses are had of the most beautiful views, ever changing, ever glorious. No one can describe them, for words fail ; but how we enjoyed them, and how often we returned to feast our eyes and tried to impress upon our memories their beauty, even taking a last walk in the rain rather than miss it !

Set close against the steep side of a cleft in the larger mountain is the upper reservoir, having the same arrangement of tanks and the same beautiful water to fill them, only, instead of the water entering by an unseen pipe, it literally comes tumbling down from cloudland in tiny rushing streams, which are filled each day by showers from the clouds that strike the mountain sides or gather about its head and fall in gentle rain. Close by a steep narrow path leads down into Larangeiras, or Orange Valley, which is long, narrow, and filled with pretty houses and villas, while the *bonde* line that runs through it passes most of the hotels, which reminds me of our hotel, said to be one of the best, and, judging by all we saw, it was.

It was two-storied, with a large entrance hall. A small office on the left, and on the right the big low-ceiled dining-room, where we enjoyed fresh shrimps and other dainties, surrounded by palms in pots, feeding two or three tame mice that came regularly to beg, and watching the natives,—their table manners being very good. There was a large *patio* behind the hall, filled with trees, roses, and plants, and around this *patio*, on the upper floor, ran a balcony closed in with blinds. Between this balcony and the street were most of the rooms, some large, some small, but the ceiling of all about fourteen feet high. The floors were bare, the furniture good, but none of it matched the bedstead, guiltless of springs, while the pillows were stuffed with a sort of cotton gathered from trees, which made them so hard that your ears ached in the morning. The windows all opened to the floor, each of those on the street having a little balcony. There were wooden shutters to them, but no frames with glass. It was always too warm to shut your room up, and the rain seldom beat in; it just fell straight down and soon ceased. The doors had shutters in them to give better ventilation, while everything was neat and clean.

Among the many beautiful mountains that encircle the bay and city, two seem to stand out prominently, and, catching the eye day after day, claim your attention. Both are peculiar in shape, and their names are descriptive. First comes Pan de Azucar, or Sugar-loaf, its great gray cone of rock sticking up smooth and pointed, like an old-time sugar-loaf after the wrapping of indigo paper was removed. Its precipitous sides are so difficult to scale that only hair-brained people attempt it. Others are satisfied to admire from a distance and enjoy the contrast the bare rock makes with the tropical forest of the surrounding peaks. The other was Corcovado, or the Hunchback, which bade us good-morning every day when we opened our windows. On the summit is what looks from below like a tiny open building, with a pagoda-shaped roof. Near the summit was a terrace, along which we sometimes saw a short train of cars making its way.

The city station for this railway is near the upper end of Larangieras Valley, a nice little building with a pretty garden in front. The trains, which run up and down several times a day, consist of an engine and a windowless car, with seats running across it. The track has three rails, the outer ones smooth and the inner one cogged. The trains run very slowly and the slight jar that the cog-wheel makes fitting into the center rail is very disagreeable. Otherwise the ride is a delight. There are two stations, and at the first one, named Sylvester, the cars stop on such a steep incline that there are slats nailed on the station platform to keep passengers from slipping as they walk along it.

The second station, near the summit, is called Peinares. Here there is a small hotel, with a pretty garden and a

shooting gallery. It takes an hour to make the trip up,
the grade being sometimes nearly 45 degrees, and the summit 2,300 feet above the sea. Naturally, the train goes
slowly, but it is not half slow enough; one would like to
crawl through these beautiful forests, so as to see more of
their beauties and wonders; the beautiful, strange trees,
some of immense height and girth, some a mass of blossoms; foliage of all shades of green, from silver white,
like our poplars, to the glossy blue-green of the magnolia
grandiflora. The trunks are round, triangular, small, large,
straight and smooth, crooked and gnarled; here, so close
together that they twine around one another; there, far
apart; some have every branch half covered with orchids of
many varieties, while others are draped with Spanish moss
or are clean as if polished. There are gorgeous blossoms on
the orchids, and some of the vines boast lovely ones, too.

These vines are quite a feature of the forest. They are
so numerous and so graceful; one enterprising cabinetmaker
in the city collected pieces of over 100 varieties, and polish-
ing the cut ends, made mosaic tops for two tables. One he
presented to the emperor, and he keeps the other in his
show-room. It is a beautiful piece of work, some of the
vines showing different colors in their stems and odd growths.
The floor of the forest is carpeted with green plants, especially ferns, in the greatest variety, from the delicate pale

green, tiny leaves on hair-like stems to the grand tree-fern with a great whorl of delicate leaves, six and seven feet long, springing from the soft brown trunk, which sometimes grows to a height of ten or twelve feet.

There are glorious views of mountains, valleys, and bays through the trees, so, when the train stops, just below the summit, every one eagerly hurries up the few remaining feet, anxious to reach the little house and have an uninterrupted view. When the house is reached it proves to be a large circular iron pavilion, built by the railway company for a restaurant, but it did not pay and has been abandoned. Custom was too irregular, as, on days when Corcovado is partly or entirely hidden by clouds, of course no one ascends to get the view, and cloudy days at the summit are very numerous. A few feet below the building a point of rock juts toward the sea on the precipitous side of the mountain. It is protected by an adobe wall, and from here one gets the view he has come so far for.

To the east, away down below, close to the base, lay part of the city and the botanical gardens; farther out, the harbor's mouth, with its two ends of the inner circle of mountains, some green islands outside, one with a light-house on it; and then the blue sea, stretching away to the horizon; to the north the main part of the city, the long, narrow part of the harbor, which was mistaken for a river by the first discoverers and called January River—Rio de Janeiro—the islands in it and the town of Nictheroy on the farther side; to the west a range of mountains, close at hand, hid all but the peaks of the far-off ranges and their own lovely woods; to the south the ranges of mountains extending down the coast, some outlying islands, and the sea.

We gazed untired until the shrill whistle of the engine called us back to the train, which went down slowly until it reached Peinares. Here it waits for the train coming up, and gives time for a cup of coffee in the pretty garden, a good long look at the eastern view, and a stroll along a road in the forest, by the side of which grew wild, double white roses and ferns in profusion. I wonder why it is that people who have been to Rio always rave over the botanical gardens, to the exclusion of all other natural beauties. Is it because those avenues of palms make such beautiful photographs? It is a lovely spot, with stretches of greensward, rare trees, plants, and orchids. It is set close at the foot of a mountain, and the gardeners wage eternal warfare against the forest to keep it from encroaching. There are walks shaded by bamboo hedges, that meet in a graceful arch overhead, and then there are those three royal avenues of royal palms, straight and tall, each silvery white trunk rising from its bed of green sod, its graceful tuft of leaves, like long uncurled ostrich plumes, moving softly in the breeze. They are wonderfully beautiful after one has learned to appreciate palms, and forgotten that Mark Twain said a palm tree looked like an umbrella struck by lightning—and here one is introduced to them in a striking manner, for, after leaving the *bonde*, we enter at a large, fine gateway and straight before us is the main avenue. To the right and left stretch the two side avenues, making a letter T. There were numbers of butterflies flitting about, but no flowers, at least but a few, and how one misses them! To a botanist or forest student the place would be entrancing, but as an ordinary traveler, who enjoys best what suits his individual fancy, I prefer the wild forest.

VI.

RIO DE JANEIRO.

IT IS A CLEANLY CITY, TOO—PECULIARITIES OF ITS HORSE-
CAR SYSTEM—STREET VENDORS AND HOW THEY CRY
THEIR WARES—THE POLICEMAN'S WAR-WHOOP AND
WHAT IT MEANS.

LIKE an undulating, curving ribbon of white jewels,
between the emerald green of the forest-covered mountains
and the deep blue waters of the bay, lies the city of Rio de
Janeiro. Surely never had a city so lovely a site before; the
glorious sweep of magnificent mountains around its bay, with
farther ranges showing behind them, until the pipe-like peaks
of the Organ range show blue and shadowy in the far distance.
Everywhere that your eye turns, whether you are on the blue
bay or ashore, a lovely picture of mountains, forest, blue
waters, and gleaming white houses greets you. And the
forests that cover these mountains! They are ideal; not only
because of their beauties, their strangeness, and rich coloring,
but also because of their accessibility; because one can walk

about in them, enjoy the trees, flowers, ferns, and numberless strange growths, as well as those that are familiar to us, and bring a breath of homesickness with their forms, reminding us of the distance we have come and the time of exile before us. Happiest when warmest, I have always longed for and dreamed of the tropics, but I never found the ideal tropics until we arrived in Rio. No wonder that imperialism lingered there; its last stronghold on this continent. Nowhere else had it such a city, such a crown of mountains, and such a convenient harbor to sail from when the day of reckoning came.

Our first evening ashore was spent in the large fine theater of Dom Pedro II., listening to " Hamlet " given by an excellent Italian dramatic troupe.

I was surprised at the cleanliness of the city. It may not be properly sewered, but it is clean, and a great many of the streets are wide. All are well paved, with good sidewalks, and there is a most excellent street car service. There are three kinds of street cars—the open ones, nicely painted and appointed, in which one pays ten cents for a ride, and must have shoes and stockings on. The second-class or barefoot cars, which are closed, have a tariff of five cents for a ride. These cars run on regular routes and follow the rails laid down in the streets. The horses and mules are good, and there are enough of them to draw the cars, so it is not necessary

for the drivers to beat them, and the company does not allow
the men to have whips. Crowding is not allowed, and
when a car is full, it will not stop for any one. The third
class is a kind of open car mounted on big wheels, and they
all seem to start from the large market down on the wharves
at one side of the Praca da Marinhas. They have a destination
which is announced on a little board which the conductor
hangs on to the roof before starting. They also seem to
have regular routes, but leave them at the request of any
passenger. These carry the lowest classes, chiefly slaves and
street vendors with their heavy packages or baskets.

These street vendors are a great institution, and I suppose
the street traffic grew up when women were so strictly confined to their houses, and now these peddlers are almost
entirely depended upon for household supplies. It is quite
the proper thing to hang out of the window or lean over the
edge of your balcony all the afternoon to watch the passers-by.
We took to it most kindly, and as strangers took a certain
amount of latitude and spent nearly all day on our balconies,
enjoying the soft, warm air, the view of Corcovado mountain
and life in the streets.

When merchandise is carried in baskets they are hung by
ropes to either end of a pole, and the pole balanced on one
shoulder. Meat is carried either in these or on a shallow tray,
fish in baskets, and vegetables the same. The different sized

fish are put in different sized baskets, and these are piled on top of one another in two piles before being attached to the pole. The largest fish are in the top basket, and I often watched a vendor separate his baskets until he reached the bottom one, where the fish were scarcely more than minnows, to sell some to an old man who had a shop opposite to our hotel and bought fresh fish every morning for his two pet cats. It was great fun to watch him do his morning marketing. Such a fuss as he and the vendor would make over the purchase of a bunch of turnips, a few red peppers, or some tiny tomatoes. They would argue, quarrel, scream, and pull the contents of the baskets all about. He would run down everything the man had and the man praise everything, until finally a bargain would be struck and the money, which seldom amounted to more than a few cents, handed over. He spent quite as much on his cats as on himself. Chickens are carried in covered baskets, and so are pigeons, while turkeys are driven in droves by one or two boys, armed with light bamboo sticks.

Each peddler has his own peculiar cry, so that one could tell what was being carried past without going to the window. There is the tin man, who strikes an iron spoon against a small tin basin as he walks, and the soap man, who raps the side of a box that he carries on his head with a stick and calls out, "Soap! Soap!" The dry-goods men have their wares in small tin trunks that are painted bright colors.

Sometimes they carry three and even four of them on their backs, bending almost double beneath the weight. If well to do they have a slave to carry their trunks—or at least used to —and walk ahead of him, calling attention by slapping a jointed yard-stick together at every step. Cobblers go about and collect shoes that need mending, stringing them all on a piece of twine, and, after a few days, they bring them back in good order.

Negroes pass along with trays balanced on their heads which are filled with candy done up in tissue paper of different colors. This candy is made in private houses—often by the ladies—and the negroes must bring back a certain amount of money for each piece sold. Whatever they make over that they are allowed to retain. It is generally in the form of yellow transparent balls that have no especial flavor and are warranted to last a long while, as biting them is impossible. These balls are all the candy one can get in the city except stale imported French candied fruits.

Instead of milk wagons cows are driven about the streets, each cow having a muzzled calf tied to her tail and a bell tied to her neck. This latter announces her approach and brings the servants to the doors and gates with bowls or pitchers, and one little French baby, that lived near us, always came out to see his cow and say good-morning to her. Slippers which are far too narrow and about half the length of the foot

take the place of shoes with the lower and middle classes.
There is no heel piece, and consequently at every step the
heel of the slipper taps the sidewalk, and this noise, while slight,
is so continuous that the ear marks it and it soon becomes
one of the familiar sounds that one grows accustomed to.

As a startling diversion, at times, there comes an unearthly
yell from the policeman on guard outside the station. At
first we took it for the announcement of a discovered murder,
but it proved to be a simple request to be relieved—a vocal
statement that his time was up and he was tired of trudging
up and down with a heavy gun and bayonet. A few moments
after the war-whoop sounded another policeman would saunter
out, take a musket from the rack near the door and take the
place of number one. A different scream turned the guard
out when any cabinet officer passed. The cabinet officers
were always to be told by two mounted orderlies that followed the carriage of each one.

Mules are quite as much used as horses; they look quite
nice and seem to have fully as much spirit, if one may judge
by the number of runaways.

If one wishes to call the attention of any one in the street or
a waiter in a restaurant one makes a long, low, hissing noise,
which seems to attract attention much more quickly than
our halloo.

We would hardly think of going to a tinsmith at home for

a trunk, but that is what one must do here, and they give you a very gorgeous article for your money. As a rule the tin is left unpainted inside and all the artist's attention given to the outside. The favorite shades for the body color are rose pink and pale blue; a bunch of flowers or a landscape covers half the lid and each of the four sides is similarly decorated. It makes conspicuous luggage, to say the least, and as the trunks are small, a family requires a great number and the sight of a family going to the railroad station, their bodies piled inside and the trunks outside, is quite astonishing.

Immense loads are carried on their heads by the porters. Six men will pick up a piano, set it on their heads and jog off with it, keeping perfect step and carrying their necks erect under what looks like a crushing burden. Chairs—piles of them—marble-top tables, wardrobes, all sorts of heavy things are set on their heads and generally there are only two men to a load. It makes one's neck ache to watch them.

It is always warm weather, so the poor dress in thin cotton clothes and they seem to enjoy life and be a jolly set, but I suppose it is because only the fittest survive, as I am told that the death rate among infants is from 70 to 80 per cent., but that once one reaches thirty years of age one is generally certain of long life. There are many fine public buildings, especially the custom-house and post-office on the First of March Street.

The houses are pretty because they always have a garden filled with blooming plants and palms, and anything would look pretty in such a setting, otherwise I did not admire them.   The rooms are good sized, and furniture made from the fine natural woods is much used and very handsome.

VII.

RIO DE JANEIRO.

THE HOTELS OF TIJUCA—FINE SUBURBAN SCENERY—THE
NEW PALACE—AN INTERESTING MUSEUM—CURIOUS MAR-
RIAGE CUSTOMS—THE STATUS OF MARRIED WOMEN.

OUVIDOR is the name of the brilliantly lined alley, which
is called a street, and is the fashionable shopping place in
Rio. It is so narrow that carts are only allowed along it
very early in the morning, and during the remainder of the
day people walk about in the street or on the sidewalk at
will. There are many gas-pipe arches across it at intervals,
so that it may be well illuminated, and it is well paved.
The shops are the finest in the city, mostly kept by French
people, and full of articles from Paris. Two corner stores
make a fine display of diamonds, and here one has the
privilege of buying native stones for a little more than they
cost in New York. One store is filled with curiosities and
native work, baskets from Minas, carved gourds, feather work

from the Amazons, humming birds, all kinds of beetles—in short, a great variety of articles. A great many shops have beautiful photographs of the wonderful scenery in and about the city, but they, like everything else in the stores, are excessive in price, so one does not buy much even after becoming accustomed to the money.

At first to see an ordinary article marked 10,000 reis staggers one until it is translated into $5! They speak only of reis, and it takes twenty of them to make one of our cents, besides the exchange in our favor, which makes them a little less. There is quite a large plaza at one end of the Ouvidor, named San Francisco, with a fine, large church facing on it that we never could find open. In the center of the garden is a statue which, I was told, was erected to honor the Thomas Jefferson of Brazil. It has gas-pipes leading all about the pedestal for purposes of illumination. Only a block away is another large plaza, with a fine colossal equestrian statue of Dom Pedro in the center. Around the base are four bronze groups representing the rivers of Brazil, composed of one or more of the Indians that inhabit the banks and fish for turtle that live in the waters. You will find a picture of it in *Harper's Magazine* for November, 1887, page 901. The writer evidently got his pictures, as well as his facts, somewhat mixed. From the plaza—or largo in Portuguese—of San Francisco all the car lines for the northern part of the

4

city start, and quite early one morning we started from there for Tijuca, which divides the honors with Petropolis as being the favorite resort in summer for the people of Rio, and is only a few miles distant in the mountains.

Petropolis entertains the court in summer, but in winter there is nothing there and it is not easily accessible, whereas the nearness to the city and lovely scenery fills the hotels at Tijuca all the year round. The streets in the northern section are the narrowest in the city; the private houses are not as good as a class, but there are many storehouses and factories, especially those for furniture. The first sign of the approaching country is the gradual enlarging of the gardens about the houses, and finally they merge into farms, with the half-ruined, neglected look that is so common in the tropics, where vegetation is so rank and rapid in growth that it is almost impossible to keep a trim garden or yard. There were a good many fine houses and some that were anything but fine, yet the vegetation veiled and hid defects until every one seemed inviting and beautiful. At the base of the foot-hills our two mules were changed for four, and our driver with an ordinary whip, for one with excellent lungs and a whip, the lash of which was longer than the car.

Under their combined influence we spun along for a short time, and at the end of the route found a vehicle something between an omnibus and a diligence waiting. Every one

GROUP OF PALMS, PARA, BRAZIL.

clambered into it, horses were brought out from the stable, and
with their aid we began to climb the beautiful mountain side.
There were the same lovely forests about us as on Corcovado.
The ferns, palms, vines, orchids and flowers; the soft, warm,
yet exhilarating air; beautiful views of valley and sea, framed
by the trees about us; a good road which rang with the horses'
footsteps; here and there a country residence, an occasional
stream leaping down toward a valley; everything the eye
rested on was beautiful. We crossed the summit of a mountain,
and driving down a little way, came to Whyte's Hotel, which
is a collection of large adobe buildings set on a terrace close
in among the mountain peaks, with a ravine in front through
which rushes a pretty stream, its noise filling the still, clear air
all night and day. The ravine is spanned by several bridges,
one of them leading to a path bordered by sweet violets, which
ends at the broad piazza in front of the original hotel. This
piazza is so wide that it is furnished, and forms the favorite
lounging place of guests. The balconies out of our rooms
overhung the brook, and we sat there for some time enjoying
the scene, until it was cool enough to walk; then we went a
long way down one of the roads, passing through a tiny village,
and being invited into his orange grove by a man who allowed
us to pick all the fruit and flowers we wanted. The views
were beautiful and extensive, while we filled our hands with
delicate ferns and wild flowers.

Returning to the hotel, we climbed one of the peaks back of it, and leaving the narrow path, went quite a distance into the forest, enjoying the views and growths so much that we only waited for the moon to rise, after dinner, before we were off again. In the new light everything looked different and still more beautiful, if that were possible. I wish I could describe it to you, but one who has never spent a moonlight night in the tropics could form no idea of it from any words at my command, it is all so entirely different from our scenery at home—not one familiar object. And here, near Rio, the very stars are different from those that watch over us at home ; here we have lost the " dipper " that points to the north star, and in its place two brilliant points of gold lead your eyes to the bright, one-sided Southern Cross.

Early next morning we were obliged to return to the city, but had a lovely ride through the forest in the fresh morning air, and noticed, as we neared the city, the new palace, surrounded by extensive grounds, so a few days afterward we went out to see what the place was like. The palace itself is a large, square, two-storied building, not an imposing structure at all. There are large iron gates for official visitors, but they are only used on such occasions as the family generally use one of the small side doors. The building is light yellow in color, and so is the small guardhouse for the company of soldiers which stands a short distance away at the head of the broad avenue which leads up from the entrance gate. Between this guard-house and the palace is a large circular graveled space. The house and grounds were bequeathed to the Emperor by a rich Portuguese, and the grounds could be made lovely if enough money was spent on them.

Here and there are a grassy slope, an avenue of trees or bamboo, and a grotto with a small lake ; but there are also so many rough, weedy, uncultivated spots that there is no effect: each view is spoiled. Quite a nice beginning for a zoological garden is in one place, half hidden by trees, the monkeys and leopards being especially fine. The interior of the palace we never saw, as ordinary visitors are not admitted when the family are there, and we were obliged to leave the city two days before the one set for our presentation on the diplomatic reception night. Santa Anna Park pleased me more than any of the others, perhaps because it is more like Central Park glorified. The stretches of greensward, lakes, fountains, bridges, clumps of trees and blooming shrubs, peacocks strutting about, pretty ducks in the lakes, and comfortable benches in the shade, all made a lovely spot to walk about and lounge in.

The city museum faces the park ; it is a large building, with most interesting collections in it. There were great numbers of well-mounted stuffed birds, quite a good showing of monkeys, a fair lot of fish, and some very curious minerals, while the collection of Indian articles, which filled two large rooms, was unusually fine and interesting. There were various curious arrows with wooden, stone, and iron heads, but the shaft generally of bamboo; tall, slender bows, canoes, shields, models of huts, and much gorgeous feather work, a mantle and many head-dresses, whose long ends must have reached to the heels of the savage chieftains. The wands, which were said to be those of office, were long and slender, covered entirely with feathers, generally of a brilliant red.

There were numbers of dried human heads, which are the scalp-locks of many tribes of South American savages; they cut the head off their late enemy and take all the bones out through the neck, then they dry and tan it over a small mould, filling the nostrils so that they stand out, and closing the eyelids; they are perfectly black and seem to become like leather, the long hair is left on and fancy knotted strings put through the lips. There is one of these heads in the Gibb's collection of Peruvian articles in the Metropolitan Museum in Central Park. There were curious burial pots of red earthenware from the Island of Marajo, rudely shaped—an attempt at the human form—about two and a half feet high. The bones are packed in them in a sort of cement or clay, and to get them in such a small place they must remove every bit of the flesh.

One good-sized case was filled with articles seized quite

recently by the police of Rio, in two or three raids which were made among the negroes to break up idolatry, and they were found using these articles in their form of worship. They were mostly cloths, knives, and beads, as the idol would generally disappear, some one secreting it quickly, but there were two figures, rudely carved out of wood, and both about two feet high. One had a bowl on his head and looked quite peaceful, while the other had his right hand raised, and a knife in it as if about to strike.

Near our hotel was one of the numerous pretty parks, facing which was a large, fine church, surrounded by a garden and approached by a fine flight of steps. On the pediment was a large bas-relief of a scene in Heaven. God, seated on a throne, is leaning forward to place a crown of roses on the head of the Virgin Mary, who kneels in front of him, while angels and saints stand about in groups. The interior decorations are simple, but fairly good, and arranged so as not to interfere with the fine proportions of the interior. It is a favorite church for weddings, and very numerous are the wreaths and bouquets of artificial orange-blossoms that adorn the different altars, placed there as offerings by brides.

A number of carriages, lined with white, and drawn by white horses, passing the hotel, meant a bridal party, and if we went at once to the church were in time to see the ceremony. Once or twice sufficed, however, as there are no bridesmaids, nor any pretty procession and group about the altar. The bride wears white; the rest of the female members of the family and friends leave their bonnets at home and wear their Sunday gowns. The groom and other men wear evening dress, and the whole party cluster pell-mell about the altar and watch the knot tied. The bride is supposed to be supported by a married friend whom she asks to take charge of her, but everybody takes charge of everybody, and the finale is a grand kissing-time. All the men kiss the groom, the women the bride, and then they kiss indiscriminately. They marry very young, the brides averaging from twelve to sixteen, and a woman of twenty is quite an old maid. They have large families, and the women pass their lives in their houses and gardens.

It is only a few years since they began to go out upon the street without the attendance of husband, father, or brother, and even yet the very best families keep their women much secluded. If a gentleman calls on a lady, she will not receive him unless her husband is at home, and some ten years ago every man, when he left his house, locked the gate and took the key with him, and his family was thus confined to the house and garden until his return; and some years before that, if he went into the country for a trip, he took his wife to a large convent near the public gardens, gave her to the nuns to keep, taking a receipt for her, and when he came back he gave up his receipt and got his wife.

RIO DE JANEIRO, BRAZIL.

Things are gradually changing for the better, as far as the treatment of women is concerned; they begin to marry a little older, and thus have a chance to get a little education of all kinds, and are better fitted to be companions to their husbands. They are also allowed more liberty, and consequently behave better; their freedom is coming slowly, but surely. They seem intelligent, and more than willing to learn the few accomplishments they are taught. They have good figures, and a good many handsome faces look at you from the balconies and gardens. The men are short in stature and dark—a great deal too dark sometimes, as there seems no objection to negro blood among the Brazilians. One of the cabinet, I was told, was two-thirds negro. The dislike to such blood seems stronger in the States than anywhere else.

There was said to be an epidemic of small-pox, and every day the papers contained quite a list of deaths from it, while any number of funerals passed the hotel, but they were almost entirely children who had never been vaccinated, or persons who had exposed themselves in the slums. We never saw a person who had recently had it. In short, people were more scared than hurt. The funerals were varied, from the tiny baby in the scarlet coffin, unattended, to the large purple velvet gold-trimmed box, buried in flowers, and followed by a long file of carriages headed by a coach that belonged to the imperial family, and sent as an empty compliment to the cast-off body of the

Emperor's faithful follower. The coffins are long, narrow, shallow boxes of wood, over which are nailed red cloth for children and purple for other people. The cover is a wedge-shaped frame, over which cloth is stretched and nailed, making a flimsy, queer-shaped coffin. In cases of extra display all the edges are bordered with gold lace.

The idea of a funeral wreath seems to be to have it as large as possible, with long streaming bows of ribbon tied to it. They are often made of artificial bead or feather flowers in spite of the abundance of natural beauties. The hearses are gorgeous, especially those for children, which are painted scarlet, while those for grown people are black and shiny, with tufts of black plumes on the roofs and on the horses' heads. Only men follow the body, in carriages, except in the case of young children, when their playmates seem to go too, and carry bunches of fresh flowers. There were too many deaths from contagious diseases to make a visit to the cemeteries other than foolhardy, so I never saw an interment.

VIII.

THE RIO DE LA PLATA.—MONTEVIDEO.

THE STREETS AND HOUSES OF THE METROPOLIS—A CITY OF
PRETTY GIRLS—CURIOUS DOMESTIC AND SOCIAL USAGES—
HOW THE COOKING AND LAUNDRY WORK ARE DONE.

WITH deep regret we said farewell to lovely Rio, and standing on the deck of the steamer, southward bound, our little
group watched, in the silence of sorrow, its beauties one by one
fade from our view—the city, harbor, mountains—all vanished,
and when we finally turned about to go below, the coast only
showed as a low-lying cloud on the horizon. Yet we had the
comforting assurance that we should once again visit this
Garden of Eden, for, in this part of the world, if all roads do
not lead to Rome, all steamship lines do go to Rio, and on our
way home we were sure to stop there.

The next day we wished ourselves back more vehemently
than ever, for heavy black clouds came rolling up from the
southwest, with every now and then a brilliant flash of lightning darting through them, and by contrast intensifying their

blackness. On they swept, and we soon were dancing, tumbling, and rolling about in the midst of a pampero; the rain passed quickly, and then the wind blew a gale for three days, and we were well inside the mouth of the Rio de la Plata before we found weather and water to suit every one.

The Rio de la Plata always seemed to me more of an estuary than a river. Its water is muddy, and there is a strong, steady current, but there is such a vast expanse of water that one does not notice the current, and when one can navigate a river for forty-eight hours without seeing land on either side, or in fact anywhere on the horizon, one needs to be a navigator to know where he is, or else to have a believing spirit to accept what is stated as a fact.

The first glimpse we had of land was of the Lobos Islands, two low, rocky islets surrounded by dangerous reefs, and getting their name of Lobos—seal—from the fact that they are a great resort in winter for seals that come up from the south and breed there in quantities. A certain number are taken every year, and there are buildings on the larger island for curing skins and trying out oil, and a corral of stout logs into which the animals are driven to be killed with clubs. The killing season is from May 15 to October 15, and the average take is 14,000, for which the government receives $10,000, and the port of Maldonado a certain amount of skins and oil to the general value of about $3,000.

On account of the seals no lighthouse is allowed on the islands, and many ships are wrecked on their reefs, but the government of Uruguay prefers its income to saving the merchant marine of other nations from disaster.

Uruguay—or, as it is officially called, Republica Oriental del Uruguay, from its being on the oriental bank of the river—is a small but wonderfully fertile and rich country, which only needs more people, law, and order to flow with milk and honey.

In the northern and eastern parts there are mountains, and the rest is what looked to us, with our memories of Brazilian mountains, a dead, monotonous level, but in reality it is a rich, rolling plain, covered with fine succulent grasses, on which the herds of cattle thrive and fatten. One never gets to the mountainous regions, because there is no grand river highway to lead people and commerce to them, and they are comparatively undeveloped. Only a few adventurous spirits or miners take the long stage coach and horseback rides, and the reports they bring back are not such as to tempt one, yet they report the country as beautiful and the mines rich. In short, the little republic can boast of a well-watered land, rich soil, good climate, and fine landscapes ; in fact, it is a land where every prospect pleases and only man is— well, he is not exactly vile, but certainly not pleasant to live with, for his ways are not ours. A republic in name and without some of the bad features of a monarchy, but personal politics, arms at the polls, good laws badly enforced, revolutions, and a

state church, all combined, make anything but an ideal republic.
Of course I am now speaking of the people as a nation, for in-
dividually the *gente decente*, or better. class, are delightful.
Their country is still young and they had a bad start. Fancy
what our country would have been if only the poorer class of
Spaniards had settled here and intermarried with the Indians,
and we had only these people to form our republic!—what a
fine mess we should have made of it!--instead of which we had
English, Dutch, French, and Spanish blood and all sorts of
creeds, each one holding the other in check and forming a common front against the Indians, and then when we had formed
the nucleus of a nation and accomplished our independence, in
our hour of need we had patriots and statesmen to start us on the
right road, and we have grown until our nation is the guiding
star of all republics and a menace to all monarchies.

On the morning of our sixth day out from Rio we arrived at
Montevideo, and what a peculiar picture it was that greeted us
as we came on deck to see the city. Everything was gray: the
sky covered with heavy gray clouds, the city of gray adobe, the
water breaking against the shore, the surrounding country, all
gray, and looking so cold and dreary. The chill wind of early
spring whistled through the rigging, and we got ashore as soon as
possible to look for something cheering, as this was to be our
headquarters for several years.

The city is built on a long, low point of land shaped

something like a whale's back, having the river on one side and the bay on the other. The bay is semicircular and shallow, large vessels having to lie a great distance from the wharves, and, as the water is liable at any time to be blown into foaming billows by strong winds, for about nine months of the year landing and shipping cargo is uncertain and risky, and it was no uncommon thing for naval officers to be detained several days on shore who had only intended stopping for a dinner or a dance, so a man living in his evening togs at the hotel was no unusual sight.

On the point of the bay opposite the city is the mount from which the city gets its name of Montevideo, or Mount Isee. It is a bare, grass-grown hill, with an old fort and lighthouse on its summit, while at its feet cluster the houses and saladeros of the suburb known as Cerro. The wharves are good, and lead directly up to the narrow streets of the old part of the city, which is built on the point. As I said before, the wind was cold, so every one stepped along briskly and there was color in their cheeks, quite cheering to look at after the pale faces of Rio; and oh! how pretty the Montevideo girls are! especially when about fifteen or sixteen; such plump little pigeons, with large dark eyes, sweet smiles, and perfectly-fitting gowns—a little too fond, perhaps, of covering their pretty skins with cosmetics, but very pretty, sweet, and attractive, all the same.

The streets are paved with gray stones, the narrow sidewalks covered with gray flagging, the houses built with thick, heavy walls made of rough kiln-burnt brick and covered with gray adobe both outside and in. The inner walls are generally frescoed with some arabesque design in colors that are put on with the aid of stencil-plates. The majority of the edifices are one story in height, although many of the modern ones boast of two and even three.

The Italian workmen model and carve the stucco until some of the fronts look like masses of beautiful stone carving, while only the poorest are quite without ornament of this kind. Often the foundation, or all the basement, is faced with slabs of marble, while the steps, door and window frames are of the same material. The windows have heavy gratings over them, and generally a venetian blind between the grating and sash.

The doors are heavy and solid, and the big bolts to secure them, like those on the windows, are heavy and clumsily made. The door, which is generally the only entrance and exit, is ordinarily put on one side of the street front of the house, and leads into a hall. The rest of the street front is taken up by a big room, which is used for the parlor. The hall is as long as this room is deep, and terminates in a patio or open court, which may or may not have a glass roof—usually not. In this front patio is the aljibe—cistern—which receives its water from the flat roof. It is made as ornamental as possible, with pretty blue and white tiles around and an arch of fancy iron work over it. In the center of the arch hangs a chain, to which is attached a bucket. The floor of the patio is of marble or brick, and many pots of flowers and plants cluster about the walls. From here doors lead into the different rooms, and these doors are partly of glass, as through them comes all the light and air that the rooms get, there being no windows. Behind this front patio there is another, connected by a passageway; out of this open more rooms and the kitchen, which is a small, dark place like a closet. At one end is a tiled shelf, in which are sunk two or more small, grated iron baskets. These are from four to six inches square, and in them the fire for cooking is made, wood and charcoal alone being used.

It is a study to one used to our stoves and ranges to see how many courses a cook will prepare over those tiny fires. I have watched them with admiration. Bread and cake are bought of the baker, but occasionally, in the country, one sees low round ovens built in the yard, and in these a fire is made, the ashes raked out, and the bread baked, as our grandmothers had it done.

Laundry work is not done in the house, so the clothes are given to an ironing woman, who sub-lets the washing part to a washwoman, this latter taking them down to the river bank. Here she kneels down, splashes them in the river, soaps, splashes again, and then laying them in a wooden tray, or on a stone, she beats them with a wooden mallet, wielding it with all her strength, the consequence being holes everywhere, and no color left in anything that originally boasted it. Then the articles are spread flat on the shore or hung on lines close by, after which they are taken back to the ironing-woman, who eventually returns the remains to you.

The rooms of the family often have fine furniture and beautiful ornaments, but carpets outside the parlor are rare, while a fire-place or stove anywhere in the house is considered an abomination by the natives, who declare that a fire is unhealthy. In fact, their houses are built and their lives ordered strictly with a view to keeping cool, which, as they have five months of winter, during which they go about blue with cold, and give you icy hands to press, seems to the stranger like a serious mistake. When making calls, at this season, one will find whole families receiving all clad in heavy garments, the women with their hands in muffs and their pretty little slippers on foot-warmers, while the gentlemen luxuriate in overcoats.

IX.

SCENES IN MONTEVIDEO

STREETS, SQUARES, AND PLAZZAS OF THE URUGUAYAN CAPITAL
—INSIDE THE HALLS OF CONGRESS—REMINISCENCE OF
PRESIDENT SANTOS—HIS EXILE AND DEATH—THE GREAT
FESTIVAL OF CORPUS CHRISTI—OPEN SALE OF LOTTERY
TICKETS—THE VARIOUS CLUB-HOUSES.

" TWENTY-FIFTH OF MAY " is the principal shopping street
in Montevideo. It gets its name from the date of independence from Spain, and is narrow and rather gloomy during the
day, but at night gas-jets and electric lights make it brilliant.
The shops are all small, and most of the names over them are
French or German, yet the clerks in the retail stores are
Spanish and really understand nothing else. There are, of
course, shops on other streets, as " Sarandi " and the " Eighteenth of July," but " Twenty-fifth of May " is the Broadway.
The display of jewelry and precious stones, especially diamonds,
is something wonderful. They are tastefully set and well dis-

played on velvet cushions. So many of these shops are there that they seem to light up the whole street. Next in number come the exchange shops and places for the sale of lottery tickets. The lottery is a government institution, and the proceeds are used for the support of the big charity hospital on the Twenty-fifth of May Street. It built the hospital originally, and has also paid for the insane asylum, besides other smaller buildings for charitable purposes, such as lying-in hospitals. Men and boys are the chief vendors, and you are assailed by them at every corner, but especially on the plazas. There are three different lists of prizes, headed by a grand prize which is either $50,000, $25,000, or $12,500. If it is the first mentioned, a whole ticket costs $10, if the second, $5, and if the last named, a ticket is $2.50. The tickets are divided into fifths; on the face of each fifth is a list of the prizes offered, a description of the ticket to let you know what color it ought to be, and on the back the date of drawing. The vendors get 6 per cent., and they always have in their pockets an official printed copy of the numbers of the last drawing, and you constantly see people stopping them and taking tickets out of the pockets to compare with the list, and see what they have drawn. Every one buys, from the street vendors of fruits and cakes, porters, and laborers up. Drawings are frequent, and prizes are always promptly paid in silver coin.

There are several plazas, or public squares, the principal ones being Constitucion, Independencia, Cagancha, and Rincon. They are all curbed and have a flagged sidewalk around them, and there are a few trees, but beyond the trees not a blade of grass or anything green is to be seen, the whole space being covered with gravel. Stone-paved paths intersect each square, and along their sides are benches, usually occupied by gossiping groups of lottery-ticket vendors. I am told that there were formerly grass, flowers, and shrubs in the parks, but Santos, the last despot who occupied the presidential chair, wanted more money, so he had a bill passed to remove all grass, etc., from the public squares and sold the privilege of doing the work. He had many curious ways of managing things, but must have had some talents to work his way up from a stable boy to the Presidency. He undoubtedly had his assassins for private work and on a few occasions, when afraid to trust them—reputable men assured me—did the work himself. Every vacant lot in the city is inclosed by a high brick wall. He and his brother bought all the bricks in the city, also those at the kilns, and then ordered all vacant lots walled in with brick within a certain time. He was finally wounded in the face by a soldier, who tried to kill him, and went to Europe to have the wound treated. No sooner had he sailed than Tajes, his minister of war, proceeded, with a regiment on which he could rely, to the barracks, where the favorite regiment of Santos was quartered, disarmed them, and then proclaimed himself President. Next a law of expatriation was passed, and Santos never again returned to Uruguay. He spent his last days in Buenos Ayres, and every now and then we would be startled by a report that he had landed at night in some part of Uruguay or even in the city, and as that meant a revolution and fighting, it was wiser to keep out of the streets until the rumor proved false. He died in Buenos Ayres, and then the government offered his widow a man-of-war to bring his body home in state, but she refused, and brought him quietly over in a regular passenger steamer, and without parade of any kind he was laid to rest among his people. He left a widow, several children, and a large fortune. Alive, he was dreaded worse than the plague ; dead, he is forgotten.

Constitucion is often called Matriz, because the Cathedral of La Matriz—The Mother—is built on one side of it. The church is very large, even for a cathedral, and from the outside its two towers and dome look very fine. The interior is bare and unusually destitute of ornament, the only costly one being the marble tomb of a bishop, with a colossal figure of the ecclesiastic in his robes kneeling on top. The ornaments on the altars are poor, but in good taste, as are the saints' statues and painted altar pieces; an air of poverty seems to pervade the place. Across the plaza is the large municipal building, neither very imposing nor pleasing except during carnival, or on some especial gala occasion, when it is beautifully decorated by day and illuminated by night. It seemed spacious and comfortable inside, the entrance being through big doors into a square hall, off which doors on the left lead into the central police court, and those on the right into the barracks of the guard, for soldiers are on duty there all the while. Two of them with fixed bayonets stand at the foot of a broad marble staircase, which leads from the rear of the square entrance hall to the floor above. Just behind the sentinels are two strong iron gates that could be quickly swung to and barred if the legislators above needed protection.

Ascending the staircase we enter a narrow hall which runs around the square inner patio, and from which doors give entrance to the different rooms. One is occupied by the senate, and any one may attend its sittings who chooses to do so, but not too many must come at one time, as only four hard wooden benches across one end of the long, narrow room are provided for the public. These are elevated, and are reached by a few steps. A heavy wooden railing separates them from the rest of the rooms, and to this railing several small leaves hang; these, when propped up, can be used by reporters, standing in front of them, to write on. At the opposite end of the room is a large desk with a big arm-chair behind it, and in the chair sits the vice-president of the republic, as presiding officer. He was an old man with pure white hair, gray beard, and a fine intellectual face. He looked very small in the very big chair. A David

Davis would have fitted it better.   On the wall just behind him
hung an oil portrait of Gen. Artigas in full uniform, and on one
of the side walls was a similar portrait of Suarez.   They were
both patriots and mighty men in their day in Uruguay.   No
desks are furnished, and if a senator wishes to read his speech
he brings it in his hand and holds it until he goes out, or puts
it in his pocket.   I never saw more than a dozen of the nineteen
senators in their seats; they attend strictly to their business,
speak sitting in their chairs, and give their assent to any
proposition by bending forward from their waists.   Four clerks
write at four desks, and, save the scratching of their pens, the
room is very still; yet as the senators speak only for one another's benefit, and the few there are of them being at the further end of the room, it is exceedingly difficult to understand
anything.

The House of Representatives meet in a similar room in another side of the building, and it is arranged much in the same
manner, except that here there are a few more benches for the
public.   There are fifty-four chairs and always a goodly number
of members present.   They speak louder and seem generally
more democratic and noisy.

On the Sarandi side of the plaza is the magnificent new three-
storied marble-faced building of the Uruguayan Club, the effect
of which is, however, spoiled for me by giving up the ground
floor to shops.   Opposite is the unpretentious brown building

which is the headquarters of Englishmen and foreigners generally, and is known as the English Club. Shops occupy the rest of the square, and over most of them are private residences, it being not at all out of the way here to live over a shop, even the president sometimes doing so.

To see the plaza at its gayest one must go in the evenings, especially on warm summer ones, when a military band plays and numerous pretty senoritas of the city and of Buenos Ayres are sitting demurely at the tables, with papa and mamma, pretending to eat ices or drink beer, while the young men wander about speaking to those they know. On Corpus Christi day it is crowded, packed with people who assemble to see the great religious procession of the year, when all the priests and societies of the city meet together in the cathedral, and issuing from it march in solemn procession around the square, singing, carrying lighted candles, and showing to the multitude the great treasure of the country, which is a small piece of the true cross. I saw the procession one year and it was a beautiful sight. The people in the surrounding houses brought out silk hangings and embroidered cloths and hung them on the front of their houses. Every balcony was filled with people, and all in and about the plaza the people were packed so close that it seemed a sea of heads as one looked down on them—a sea that swayed and surged as each one strove to better his position. The curbstones on each side of the street were lined with soldiers in full uniform, and there was a military band at each corner. There was some delay, but finally the procession issued from the church, and it was so long that it reached nearly around the square. First came the boys destined for the priesthood, then those who were training for missionaries; next a veiled host on the top of a long pole, the veil stiff with embroidery, borne by a priest. It was followed by a long line of them; next the big white satin gold-embroidered banner of the bishop; behind that a banner of cloth of gold, with a small glass case hanging in the center of it. In this case was the piece of the true cross, and at its approach the soldiers and the people all knelt. Next came a veiled host, then a pennant, which was so heavily embroidered with gold that it stood out straight and stiff. Just behind was a double row of Jesuit priests in robes— as well as others—their candles being in lanterns. Priests of the cathedral, dressed in the robes of the mass, followed, then priests walking backward and burning incense before the bishop, who walked beneath a yellow brocade canopy, dressed in gorgeous robes and surrounded by attendants. After he passed, all those who were kneeling arose and watched the priests of different parishes, headed by veiled hosts, file by. The procession closed with numerous societies, all dressed in ordinary dress and distinguished by the ribbons around their shoulders. When all had paced slowly around the square they entered the cathedral and a long service followed, but as soon as they had disappeared behind the doors the band struck up a march, the soldiers fell into line and marched off to their barracks, while a few people went in to attend the service and the majority went home.

It was a lovely spectacle, there was so much gold, so many brilliant priests' robes, the bands playing, soldiers' uniforms glittering, the procession chanting, the bells all over the city ringing merrily, the kneeling crowd—it all looked very pretty in the bright sunshine, and to Roman Catholics, who understood the meaning of all the details, it must have been especially attractive.

Independencia Plaza is only two blocks away, and is the largest in the city. It is intended to have a colonnade all around it, but the work progresses slowly, and only the two ends and part of the sides are so decorated. It is surrounded by shops and houses, except a large public building called the Government House, which is filled with different offices, among them those of the president; and any day about four the latter could be seen to come out and enter his handsome coupe, which took him to his own house on the "Eighteenth of July Street." The 18th of July is the anniversary of the adoption of the constitution, and the street is a fine wide one, being in the new part of the city. It is planted with a row of trees on each side, and is very long, extending way out into the country. Plaza Cagancha is made by widening the Eighteenth of July Street for two squares, and contains the only statue in the city, and it is erected to Liberty. On the top of a tall Corinthian column of marble is a female figure in bronze, wearing the Phrygian cap and draped in the costume of ancient Greece; one hand holds the flag of Uruguay, and the other a pair of broken shackles. Rincon Plaza is in the old part of the town and is surrounded by small houses. It is often used as a drill ground for troops, and on summer evenings the benches are freely patronized by spoony couples, as it is not very brilliantly lighted. One of the streets which leads from it to the water is called Washington, named for our immortal George.

X.

OSTRICHES IN URUGUAY—VISIT TO SENOR SA-PELLO'S BIRD FARM NEAR PIEDRAS.

AN AFTERNOON AT THE QUIET VILLAGE OF SANTA LUCIA —A DECAYING TOWN THAT ONCE ENJOYED A BOOM--ITS BIG HOTEL AND GRASS-GROWN STREETS.

THE Central Railroad of Uruguay passes through many little towns near Montevideo, and sometimes we made excursions on it to see the hamlets and pass a day in the country away from the heat of the city. Some one told us that Santa Lucia was an interesting place, so we made it the destination of our next outing. For two hours and a half the train slowly crossed the flat country, often stopping at pretty little stations, with towns more or less near them. When quite near to Santa Lucia we caught a glimpse of a rather broad stream, called a river, with a pretty good current and quite high bluff banks for this country. Arriving, we found a railroad station large and airy, with rooms for the station-master and his family at one end, as well as a garden for his flowers and chickens in the rear. There was the usual crowd of men and women to watch the passengers alight, most of the women Indians, with a few oranges or lemons to sell. Most of the men were natives, dressed in riding costume, who had come in from their farms for pleasure or profit, and having tied their horses to the fence, were watching the travelers while patronizing the bar. A cloud of hackmen surrounded us as we stood making up our minds what to do next. They were eager and clamorous, but we told them in English we did not want anything, and finally they left us in despair. I wish now that we had gone with one of them to see where he would have taken us, and what castles in Spain he would have built out of his imagination with which to glorify the decaying little town.

Once Santa Lucia had a boom as a summer resort, and the brothers Fernandez, who had made a pile of money in the Oriental Hotel in Montevideo, decided to build a summer hotel in Santa Lucia, so as to make a second fortune, instead of which they speedily became bankrupt; and, seeing the hotel, one cannot wonder at their non-success. It is separated from the railroad depot by a broad street and a large grove of eucalyptus trees, each of which had to be brought there and set out. The building occupies a block about 300 feet square. It is built one room deep and one story high clear round. Of these rooms about forty are guest-chambers, two dining-rooms and the rest given over to servants and rubbish. When I tell you that the

AVENUE OF PALMS, BOTANICAL GARDEN, RIO DE JANEIRO.

regular price for two people in a room during the season is—with two meals a day—only $2 a head, you can easily see why this big building did not pay. The patio is a garden filled with vegetables and here and there some flowers; between them and the building was a broad bricked terrace, with columns and a roof of iron trellis thickly covered with grape-vines. It made a lovely place to walk or lounge in, and after a good breakfast we talked to a group of young girls who had come there with their families to spend the summer. They put us through a catechism and we returned the compliment, but from their account there did not seem anything of especial interest in the town, so we sat there during the heat of the day, improved our Spanish by practice, and watched the women of all ages suck *mate*, while the young fry amused themselves with a dead mouse, burying, digging it up, and throwing it around, none of them apparently objecting at all to handling it. Finally we started out and walked clear through the town several times. It is said to have 3,000 inhabitants, and it may; anyway its forlornness made it fascinating. The streets are wide, grass-grown, and silent, scarcely a creature stirring. Wild flowers grew along the roads, while here and there were clumps of elderberry bushes in full bloom.

There are a goodly number of houses with pretty little gardens about them, and in some cases people were sitting on the piazzas or in the patios, but not all could boast of inhabitants;

many were windowless, their roofs falling in or fallen, with
weeds, tall and rank, pushing their way up through the brick
pavements of the deserted rooms.   We asked a shopkeeper for
the reason ; like most foreigners of the Latin race, he first
shrugged his shoulders, and then told us he only knew that the
people who had money enough to go to Montevideo never came
back, and only those without money were left, so his business
did not flourish.   The main plaza was a shady, quiet place with
plenty of benches about under the trees and a band stand.   A
man who was busy putting a fresh coat of paint on the benches
told us he was getting ready for the summer—one month of
that delightful season had already flown—and that every other
evening a band composed of some of the youths of the town
used the stand and gave free concerts.

The church faced the plaza, and we walked in at the open
door.   It was large and the air felt cool, vault-like, and pleasant after the burning sun.   The altars already built were plain
and poor, while a statue of St. Joseph standing on a dry-goods
box had a small money box nailed up near it, with a printed
request that you contribute something toward furnishing him a
suitable altar that he might be properly worshipped.   A few
roughly-made confessionals stood near the base of the columns
that supported the roof, and a pail of water with a sprinkler in
it occupied one of them.   A small boy had been at work with
the sprinkler wetting the floor, but just then he was occupied by

a game of marbles outside, and only returned when a priest put his head out of a door near the high altar and repeatedly called " Pedro ! "   The priest retreated when he saw us, and the boy stood some time struggling with his inclination to follow us about rather than return to his work.   Chairs were standing in the center aisle in great confusion, as if the congregation had but lately left, and in front of one of them lay a tiny pair of shoes and stockings, just where some impatient youngster had kicked them off.

Walking to the river, which bears the same name as the town, we wandered for some time in a grove along its banks, picking wild flowers and admiring the pretty stream.   Here and there were fishermen, and we hoped every minute to see a finny prize hauled out ; but as none came we finally engaged an elderly disciple of Izaak Walton, with balloon breeches, in conversation.   He was an enthusiastic sport, and the yarns he spun us about the size of the fish he had hauled out of that brook would have astonished me if I had not been used to fishermen's yarns at home.   It was a lovely cool spot to stay in, so we encouraged him to talk, and imperil the future of his soul until a distant whistle warned us to make our bows, express our thanks and hurry to the station, where we found a train that whirled us back to Montevideo.

Another day we started for the town of Piedras to visit an ostrich farm near there.   There is a small ostrich—called by the

6

natives Nandu—which abound in the southern part of the
continent of South America. They are as inferior to the
African bird in feathers as in size, but have long been hunted
with the *bolas*, their skins making pretty rugs and the feathers
the finest of dusters. When tracts of land were fenced in for
the purpose of stocking with cattle a greater or less number of
these birds were confined, and the owners of the *estancias* tried
to improve the breed by importing some of the large African
birds. They would not mate, however, and the estancieros
had to content themselves with keeping an eye on the herds in
the bad seasons and seeing that only a certain number were
killed every year, for whose skins they get one dollar each, on
an average. The farm near Piedras is of African birds entirely,
and is owned by an Italian, Señor Sapello by name, who formerly raised horses, and when he heard of the Zulu war, he
filled a ship with his cattle and sailed with them for the Cape of
Good Hope. He found a ready market with the English for
his wares, and while visiting the town saw some young birds
and visited a feather exchange, and, seeing large profits in the
business, he bought a few pairs of chicks for $300 a pair, and
returning to Uruguay started the farm, which pays him
splendidly. From the station a ten minutes' drive brings one
to his gate. This the driver opens, and thence the road leads
to a second gate. This was locked, but in answer to a lusty
pull at the bell a peon came, who smilingly led us through a

grove of eucalyptus trees up to the large one-storied house, embowered in grapevines growing on iron trellises. Mr. Sapello and his two sons received us most kindly, answering all our questions with the greatest care, and seemed to feel quite repaid by the interest we took. There are now 150 pairs of grown birds all kept as near the house as possible for convenience in attending to their simple wants. All are natives of the place except the first few pairs, and several have been sold. Each pair have about an eighth of an acre to themselves, which is enclosed by a high wire fence, while inside there are several trees, grass, and a small wooden hut. They retire into the latter at night and a peon closes the door, thus securing them from prowling dogs. The trees are for shade, which seemed very grateful to them the hot day that we were there, as they not only stood in it but fanned their bodies with their wings, looking like ballet dancers with fluffily-dressed bodies and bare legs. They stand from six to ten feet high, and when the feathers are plucked so one may see the size of the body, they appear all legs and neck. The legs are entirely destitute of feathers or hair and their owners brand them on the hip. The neck has short, gray, hair-like feathers, and the large brown eyes quite redeem the small, flat head, giving them an air of intelligence. The body of the male is covered by black feathers, with long, white plumes on the wings, and gray ones on the tail. The females are gray, instead of black, and have the same plumes. They are about the same size as their mates, and each bird averages twenty-five long white plumes to a wing, besides those from the tail, and a varying number of medium length that can be taken from the body.

They lay, as a rule, two eggs a month, which are at once taken from them and placed in the incubator, which is in a long low building kept at an even temperature by hot water pipes. After ten days the egg is placed in front of a strong ray of light, when a dark spot will show if the chick is forming; if not, the egg is blown and the shell kept to give a visitor. They hatch after forty-two days, when the bird is about the size of a bantam, covered with soft brown feathers. They live in hovers a month or two, carefully fed with chopped alfalfa, and are then kept in a yard until large enough to be put out in pairs. Full growth is attained about a year after hatching, and from then on they are plucked every six months. As they are strong and pugnacious, the feathers could not be pulled without injury were the bird left free, so each one in turn is driven into a small box and the door closed behind it. Just at the height of the body there are small doors on each side, and by opening them the feathers are reached without danger, only the small ones are pulled, the others being cut off to give as little pain as possible. The feathers are boxed and shipped to a regular agent in Paris, who returns large sums for them. The birds are fed on alfalfa, never get sick, and live a long while.

XI.

CLOSING CEREMONIES OF A CONGRESS OF SOUTHERN REPUBLICS.

A NOVEL AND BRILLIANT SCENE—SOME OF THE NOTABLE PERSONS PRESENT—FINE NAVAL DISPLAY—MARKETS OF MONTEVIDEO—HOW THE POLICEMEN ARE FOUND WHEN WANTED.

FLOWERS were plenty and cheap all about Montevideo, and they were used in the greatest profusion upon all occasions. Set pieces were the favorites, and I remember the day after a wedding seeing two carts loaded with floral offerings, being sent to decorate the church that the bride attended—tables a yard or more high and as large across, easels with large shields, the whole some five to six feet high; lyres, hearts, harps, and wreaths, all of astonishing dimensions, entirely covered with lovely flowers. At funerals the hearse would be all overhung with enormous wreaths, with fluttering ribbons, on which were stamped the name of the donor, some tribute of affection or of friendship. The quintas—as houses in the suburbs and country are called—are surrounded by spaces filled with fruit trees and flowers, and the latter are plucked and worn at all times.

The grandest display I ever saw was one February day, when, by invitation, we went to the Solis Theater to see the closing ceremonies of an international congress of South American republics. The Solis is a large yellow building, set well back from the street, with a graveled space in front; and this was deeply covered with branches of eucalyptus, while the entrance steps disappeared beneath carpets. The interior is like that of most Spanish theaters. On the floor are the parquet or orchestra chairs, with five galleries rising above, the first three divided off into boxes—a grand box for the President over the door, and in one of the tiers several boxes looking like bird-cages, with gilded lattices in front, these being for the use of any one in mourning who wishes to attend the play unseen. The fourth gallery is the *cazuela*, for ladies who came unaccompanied by gentlemen, and the fifth is here called *paraiso*, or "paradise."

The theater is large and the decorations are simple, but at this time the whole interior was draped with blue and white cambric, while over these drapings were hundreds of festoons of natural flowers, row after row of them, filling the air with a delicious fragrance. The curtains of the boxes were looped back with bouquets, and on the stage, which was covered with a plain red carpet, were huge bunches of potted palms. In the rear was a large stand of arms and flags, mirrors were set about the sides, and in front was a semicircle of thirteen chairs for the members of the congress.

The audience was most brilliant. In the state box, in two large arm-chairs, sat President Tajes, of Uruguay, and President Celman, of the Argentine. The latter was the guest of the nation, having come over for this special ceremony, arriving in state, accompanied by his men-of-war, and received in great style by all the foreign ships in the harbor; but, thanks to a pampero, he was too sick to appreciate it. He is a slight, pale, colorless man, of medium height, with light brown hair, close trimmed, full beard, watery blue eyes, and expressionless face. He wore citizens' evening dress, with the national baldric of his country under his coat. Tajes was also slight, but with broad shoulders and a military carriage that showed off well his gold-embroidered general's uniform. He has jet-black eyes, hair, moustache and imperial, and sallow skin, while altogether the expression of his face was not amiable, but rather tartarish; yet it had character, and he looked twice the man his guest did. He wore the national baldric outside his coat. These dignitaries were surrounded by a glittering throng of diplomats in full uniform and military men in attendance. Most of the boxes were filled by men wearing uniforms, and the thin summer dresses of the ladies were bright in color, the whole making a brilliant setting for the two or three civilians, whose simple dress looked

strangely prominent.   Those showing most prominently, because
nearest the throne, were the Vice-President of Uruguay, and
Señor Brizuela, representative of the republic of Paraguay.

As soon as the Presidents were seated the thirteen members
of the congress filed in and took their places, Garcia Lagos,
minister of foreign affairs, in the center, with Quirna Costa on
his right.   All rose to their feet as the orchestra began the
national hymn of the Argentine, and remained so until it was
finished and the Uruguayan had succeeded it.   Then we seated
ourselves and Señor Lagos rose and read a short paper, welcom-
ing President Colman, and briefly touching upon the work of
the congress.   To all the natural dignity of his race, Señor
Lagos adds a noble face, fine voice, large body, and a mass of
longish white hair, which gives him a leonine appearance.
There was no applause when he finished.   Evidently it was not
the proper thing, as Quirna Costa, of the Argentine, who followed him with an excellent paper, also took his seat amid
profound silence.

Rising once again, we all listened to the repetition of the
national hymns, the two Presidents shook hands, and then we all
left.   No expense had been spared.

The ceremonies were short, and the whole affair was delightfully dignified; such a charming contrast to many scenes I had
witnessed at home, where noise, vehemence, and hilarity take
the place of dignity, until it really seemed as if our public men,

when assembled for business, were but a pack of schoolboys out on a lark. President Celman staid seven days in all, and was entertained all the while, the whole city enjoying a holiday. It was a pity he was too sea-sick to see his reception afloat, for it was an impressive sight.

Early on the appointed day all the foreign men-of-war in the harbor got up steam and, going outside, anchored so as to form a lane for the guest to enter the port by. A strong wind sprang up about noon, and as it was four o'clock before the Argentine fleet appeared, we were by that time bobbing about right merrily ; but the breeze blew the flags out finely and the bright sunshine showed the men manning the yards, the shining guns, and all the beauties of fighting ships to perfection. First in the procession came the three Uruguayan gun-boats, dancing along and looking like yachts with their fine lines; then the Argentine fleet, Celman on board the large iron-clad Patagones, which looks more like a fort adrift than anything else. As she passed the yards were manned, marines paraded on the quarter-deck and a national salute of twenty-one guns was fired from each ship, each gun being returned from the Almirante Brown, so for a time we had all the scenic effects of a naval battle without any of its disasters. Celman was taken ashore in an open launch, which was fitted in blue and white velvet for the occasion, and was well soaked with spray before reaching the wharf, where Tajes, a number of dignitaries, and many people were waiting to welcome him. Several balls were given, the finest being those of Saenz Pena, Argentine minister to Uruguay, and the Uruguayan Club, the latter throwing open its large new marble building on the Martriz plaza.

There are some curious scenes in the streets here, one of the most pleasing being the Sunday morning market on the Eighteenth of July Street, from Plaza Independencia to Cagancha, about one-half mile. By midnight on Saturday the carts begin to arrive, and the venders place their wares upon the sidewalk or on pieces of cloth spread upon the pavement of the street. At daylight the scene opens, and all good marketers are there to buy the fresh country vegetables, chickens, geese, kids, baskets of native manufacture, braided fans to keep alive charcoal fires, pots of red earthenware, whips of rawhide, cheap laces, wax matches sold by tiny Italians, candles and quantities of flowers in pots. The countrymen in their ponchos, the women in bright colored calicoes, the children tumbling about everywhere, and the noise of their bargaining—all is interesting, and it only lasts a few hours, for by eight o'clock the street must be cleared, and it is, every bit of rubbish even having vanished.

The policemen wear a uniform, and a sort of shako on their heads. They are armed with a short two-edged knife or sword, called a *machete*, which they do not hesitate to use when arrest is resisted. They also have whistles, which they often sound, but I did not succeed in finding out why.

I frequently saw them sitting on little stools resting, and at night they place a hand-lantern in the center of a street and stay near it, so if you need a policeman you run for the nearest lantern in the street, and there one is sure to be. Chickens are carried about in untanned round hide baskets that have covers, one slung each side of a mule, and it must be uncommonly warm and uncomfortable for them.

On every corner are found *changadores*, or porters, who wear blouses, soft fishermen's caps, and carry a piece of stout rope. They will carry anything anywhere one wishes, and charge enormously for doing so. They belong to a guild and draw $2 every day as their wages, turning in whatever they have received during the day to a collector, who visits each one every night. In the suburbs, especially near the foot of the mount, there are many saladeros, where large numbers of horned cattle are killed daily during the summer season, for the hides and flesh, the latter being made into jerked beef, quantities of which are sold to Brazil and all through the interior. They also kill whole herds of horses for their skins alone. Driving large country carts, drawn by patient oxen, whose eyes seem starting from their sockets with the pain of the heavy beam-like yoke laid upon their brains and lashed to their horns, one sees countrymen in the present dress of the native peasant. It con-

sists of shoes of canvas, with soles made of rope; very
full trousers, plaited into bands around the waist and ankles;
a woolen or cotton shirt, according to the season; any kind
of a hat, and always the poncho, which is a square of
cloth having a slit in the middle for the head to pass
through.

XII.

HOTELS IN MONTEVIDEO—THE FAVORITE BATHING RESORTS.

RAMIREZ AND POCITOS THE MOST POPULAR BEACHES—THE
BEAUTIFUL CEMETERIES OF BUCEO—STREET CAR LINES
EXTENDING TO ALL THE SUBURBS—NOTES AND INCIDENTS.

WHEN we asked for hotels in Montevideo, two were mentioned as being the very best in town, yet the way they are spoken of is unique. It seems to suggest two horns of a dilemma, and nothing else. At the Pyramides one is promised a good table and small rooms; at the Oriental, good rooms and poor table. We thought any rooms would seem large after state-rooms on board ship, so we tried the Pyramides. We found the rooms low, small, stuffy,—moldy is a better word,—the table fair; charge $3.50 a day, and the ordinary conveniences of life so badly attended to that we left in a week. Next we tried the Oriental, and spent many months there, always welcomed and sped by handsome

old Don Ramon, whose manners and Spanish made one think
of the priest he was educated for, but when you saw his
troop of children about him, and the happiness in his face
as he petted and spoiled them all, you felt the world had
gained if the Church had lost, and that he was truly happy.

His hotel is said to be the only one where a lady can live alone
without being annoyed.   However that may be, she is certainly
safe at the Oriental.   Ladies eat in the general dining-room
without being spoken to or unduly stared at.   It was built for
a hotel, is three stories and a basement in height, of brick,
covered with adobe and a yellow wash.   The blinds are painted
green, and there are numerous flagstaffs on the roof, as when
he has foreign ministers with him Don Ramon keeps the flag of
their country flying, and I have seen as many as four fluttering
in the breeze at one time.   All windows go to the floor so as to
give plenty of air, and there are cracks all around them, as well
as around the doors.   It is built on the corner of Piedras and
Solis streets, and occupies a square plot.   Inside there are four
inner courts, or *patios*, which reach to the roof, and are covered
with glass, awnings also being stretched in summer to keep out
the sun.   Around three of them are the public rooms and
guest chambers, the fourth being given up to kitchen, laundry,
and servants' rooms.   Around each one, at every story, there
runs a narrow-railed balcony, which gives access to the rooms,
and these balconies are reached by a marble staircase.   The

azotea—roof—is flat and used to dry clothes on, but on most of
the private houses these flat roofs are used as the broad piazzas
of homes in the Southern States are. The ceilings of the rooms
are high, and the floor space all one can desire. The floors are
covered with carpet, and if one looks after the chamber-maid
she will keep the room clean and the plentiful furniture dusted.

The chamber-maid is a luxury in South America, and the
Oriental only boasts of one, who has charge of all the rooms in
which there are ladies, the others being looked out for by two
men. The windows of the rooms next the street, as I said
before, reach to the floor and open on to narrow balconies ; in
summer these stand open day and night, yet one is never
troubled by the neighbors, and a robbery is unheard of. The
inside rooms, which are by far the more numerous, get light
and air through a hybrid door-window, that is, a door with panes
of glass in it. Inside, if guests wish light and air, they must
sacrifice privacy, and *vice versa.* The balconies and passage-
ways are floored with brick and the walls whitewashed. The
dining-room is on the ground floor, and receives light and air
from three glass doors into the *patio* and one into a passage,
and it was often so dark we could not see to read. The floor of
wood, inlaid, was very nice in summer ; but in winter, as there
is no fire in the hotel outside of the kitchen, one often sighs for
the warmth of a carpet, yet, noticing the native habit of ex-
pectorating, flinging cigarette stumps and matches on the floor,

one becomes reconciled to a floor that can be scrubbed. The food is good, and after one becomes used to the garlic and onions it is palatable. Onions and garlic are in every dish, and there is not the slightest use in remonstrating. Neither for love nor for money will these cooks leave it out.

I have described the Oriental at such length because it was the best we found, and because it is typical. The slipshod way in which everything was managed, no housekeeper, no head-waiter, all the servants doing as they choose, the guests putting up with everything and enjoying themselves; Don Ramon polite, smiling, always ready to pour oil on the troubled waters; the large, airy building, the whiteness of marble and white-wash everywhere, the waste of space in the *patios*, and the many dark rooms,—all were typical.

In summer the place was a beehive, for it is the fashion in Buenos Ayres to go to Montevideo for the baths, the latter city being so much nearer the ocean that the water is somewhat salt. Family after family would arrive, and the size of some of them was astonishing—papa, mamma, any number of children up to a dozen, cousins, aunts, uncles, and all sorts of relations. They would take a few large rooms and stow themselves away, only they and the chamber-maid knew how. They would fill the house to overflowing, and then the *patios* were delightful places. All were always jolly and every one did as they pleased. The pretty girls wore lovely toilets and were always ready for a chat or a walk, provided it was not a man who approached them. If one of the last-mentioned came to call they would sit as demure as kittens and let mamma or aunt do the conversing, putting in here and there a word or smile, but not many. In the early afternoon their very best frocks were donned, along with their gayest hats and prettiest jewelry, the children would grasp pail and shovel, and there would be an exodus for the bathing beaches.

There are two favorite places, Ramirez and Pocitos, either only to be reached by a long ride in the street cars. Ramirez is the nearer, and after a twenty minutes' dash along the streets, through soft warm air and clouds of dust, one arrives at a long pier, the shore end of which has a restaurant, band-stand, and little tables set about on a platform. At the other end are bath houses, with ladders leading down into the water, and these were the favorite resorts for those who could swim. On one side of the pier were a number of bathing machines, which were drawn in and out of the water by mules, and into these the pretty girls, with their dainty, gayly-colored gowns, would flock, be drawn out into water, and, when pulled in again, would emerge with everything in perfect order and their crimps intact. It was a puzzle, until I was told that they never went into the water at all, but made the excuse to go to the beach, and afterward sit around the tables, taking some light refreshment, and having their toilets and themselves admired

7

by the men, old and young, who flocked there, and who are obliged to bathe on quite another part of the beach. Of course there was a *tambo*—cow-shed. *Tambos* abounded in the city and in all the suburbs, for the natives like milk hot from the cow, and to get it they will go into a cow-shed, sit there among all the odors and flies, and drink milk which they see milked.

It takes about three-quarters of an hour to reach Pocitos, but when reached it is quite a little town, and the beach is really a good sandy one. The restaurant is on a hotel piazza, and there is a pier for promenaders. A number of people of Montevideo have country places here, but the majority of visitors stay in the city, and come down each day for their dip.

Not much farther down the coast are the cemeteries of Buceo, one used by the Roman Catholics, and the other owned by an English company and open to Protestants. They are lovely places, lying, as they do, on a slope of land with a lovely view of surrounding plains and boundless river. Then there are so many flowers, great masses of them all about, and borders, stretching down between the rows of silent dead. It is horrible to have any one we have been friendly with buried far from home, quite among strangers; but if one could ever be reconciled to it, it would be in the quiet, lovely, flower-decked cemetery of Buceo. The street-car lines extend for miles out into the country in all directions. Horses are cheap, so three or four are put to a car and driven to death. They go at a great pace, and are urged by a whip long enough to wrap around the necks of the leaders. Distances are great, but I have seen the poor beasts abused until I preferred to get out and walk. For any but the swellest funerals, and even for some of those, it is customary to hire street cars for the mourners, and one often sees a hearse, with perhaps one carriage containing the immediate family, trotting along the streets heading a procession of street cars filled with men smoking cigarettes. Women do not go to funerals, and the men are always smoking their eternal cigarettes. As a friend remarked, it was only needed for the corpse to sit up and smoke, to complete the picture and make all hands happy.

XIII.

THE CARNIVAL SEASON IN THE GAY CAPITAL OF URUGUAY.

DECORATIONS AND PROCESSIONS, THE BATTLE OF FLOWERS—
PRIVATE AND PUBLIC BALLS—AN EVENING AT THE SPANISH
CLUB—MUSIC AND OTHER ATTRACTIONS AT THE CITY PARK.

THE three days before Ash Wednesday ushers in Lent
are given over in Montevideo to the delights and license
of the carnival, but many days before that the city was
filled with preparations, and the daily papers with announcements and comments. Eighteenth of July, Twenty-fifth
of May, Sarandi, and parts of Colon streets, Independencia,
Constitucion, and Zabala plazas were decorated by the city, as
along them the daily procession was to pass. Every few feet
on each side of these streets, next the curb, a paving-stone was
removed, and one end of a long, slender, square pole driven into
the place thus made. These poles were wound with blue and
white cambric ; from pole to pole were hung rows of small bunt-
ing flags of every conceivable shape and hue. This made two

bright lines of color by day, while a row of Japanese lanterns hung under the flags and, illuminated each evening, gave color and brightness at night. Across the street arches of gas jets were placed, and there must have been several thousands of them. In the plazas there were the same decorations, an addition being the substitution of blue and white glass globes for the every-day white ones. Blue and white are the national colors, the flag being composed of narrow horizontal alternate stripes of the two colors, a white field in the upper corner next the staff having a yellow sun upon it.

The store windows all displayed a goodly assortment of *pomitos*, which are lead tubes with caps, like those that oil paints come in, only very much larger. They are filled with cheap scented water, and by giving them a good squeeze one could throw a jet of the water, with considerable accuracy, about six feet. Everything, except these and flowers, it was strictly forbidden to throw, yet we were advised to seek the seclusion of our rooms, and stay there during King Folly's reign, as dirty water and ancient eggs would be used as much as ever. That, however, was not our idea of seeing foreign people and their ways, so Sunday we put on some old clothes and sallied forth. First we took a ride around in the street cars, and saw groups of maskers in their Sunday best, all laughing and having a good time. Here and there were rooms where societies, in fancy dress, were gathering before joining the procession ; but beyond one small boy, who was filling a rubber squirt at a mud-puddle in the street, there was nothing alarming, so we got out, and, making our way to the Eighteenth of July Street, found the broad thoroughfare crowded. Prizes had been offered for the finest decorated house along the route, while in the procession the finest ornamented car belonging to a society, the best decorated carriage, the finest horses, and prettiest costume were all to be rewarded. The crowd was good-natured and merry ; the maskers were quite plenty, very few in fancy dress, nearly all wearing dominos ; *pomitos* were plentiful and freely used, the neck and face being the favorite points of attack, and woe to any one who wore eyeglasses ; they were wet as quickly as dried and the wearer helpless most of the time.

Every house has one or more balconies, which were all more or less gayly decorated, one family having brought out all their parlor furniture, hanging the curtains on the outside of the windows, the pier mirrors between, and placing ornaments here and there as they usually were displayed inside. Mounted police and soldiers tried to keep a passage-way open down the center of the street, and finally the procession came. First marched a band of music, and then the managers, mounted on fine horses ; after these many societies with bands of music here and there. The favorite dress among these associations was a species of African, consisting of plenty of black tights, fancy colored trunk breeches, anklets, armlets, wigs of long wool, a big straw hat hanging on their back by strings passed around the neck, and a tin rattle or wooden clapper in one hand.

There were numerous Italian societies and a band of bull-fighters—the bull, two men encased in an old hide—and whenever the procession halted they gave a most comical burlesque of a bull fight. One tall red wagon was filled with men dressed as butterflies, their red bodies and gracefully waving golden-gauze wings being beautiful. A band of Spanish students were noticeable ; and finally came the citizens, in carriages, headed by the President's wife, in full evening dress, the vehicle decorated with the national colors. Many of the ladies were simply in evening toilets, with tiny black velvet masks, while others were in fancy costume, some of the latter being especially striking. The battle of flowers that day was on part of the Twenty-fifth of May Street, and a great many blossoms were thrown between the balconies and carriages during the hours when it lasted. That evening the illuminations were very fine, all the gas arches and lanterns being alight, and all the public buildings outlined with tiny flames. There were crowds of people in the streets, afoot and in carriages, all good-natured, all using *pomitos*, and all having a charming time. Even the small boys, who followed every one that had a nearly empty *pomito*, so as to get the lead case when thrown away to sell, were as jolly as sandpipers, which is not generally the case, children here being too solemn and sedate as a general rule to please me.

Monday was a repetition of Sunday, except that we went in the evening to a fine ball given by the Spanish Club in their roomy quarters on the Eighteenth of July Street. All the clubs give balls every night of the carnival, and there are besides many private and public balls, but we were advised to accept our Spanish Club invitation as being the most exclusive and best club at that time. Their lofty rooms are entirely decorated in the national colors—red and gold—which make them very brilliant; and large as they were, by one o'clock they were filled to suffocation, so the fine band, hidden among palms, played dance music to no practical purpose. There were handsome toilets, but not among the maskers. Only ladies were allowed the privilege of hiding their faces, and as those who took advantage of it never uncovered them, nor removed their dominos, there was no incentive among them to fine gowns. They prefer dominos, as they cover hair, neck, and ears, making identification more difficult. Supper and fine wines were served all the evening, and one could easily see where the club spent $13,000 on their three balls.

The third evening we passed at the Italian legation, the Duke and Duchess Licignano inviting their friends and throwing open their house to receive maskers. Many of the latter came, and among them a company of Morescas, who danced an old Italian sword dance for our edification, and then we danced ourselves until Lent came in. Lent should have caused the

TIJUCA, BRAZIL.

cessation of masks and mummery, but it did not ; groups in odd
attire went about the streets, and there were balls every night
until the following Monday, when the decorated wagons—with
their flowers all faded—were brought out once more to escort
the dying King of Carnival to his grave in the Prado. A figure
lay upon a couch in one of the carts ; one doctor leaned over
him with a fan, while another stood by with a lot of instruments in his hands, but both were shaking their heads dolefully,
and by the end of the journey he was supposed to be dead, and
unceremoniously hustled into a hole in the ground. The next
day the decorations were removed, the city resumed its quiet,
gray aspect, and our ears were no longer tortured by the shrill
falsetto tones assumed by the maskers to add to their disguise.
The whole public cost was $17,000, $15,000 of which was paid
by the Government.

The Prado is a large tract of land lying in the outskirts of
the city, which was once intended for a private residence, but is
now used as a city park. It is approached under long lines of
eucalyptus trees and the grounds are prettily laid out although
far from finished. There is a sluggish stream that passes along
one side and many fine trees. A hotel and restaurant, near
which a band plays on certain days in the week, form an ending
place for afternoon drives, and one of those curving, endless
railways has lately been erected. Part of the park is fenced off
and used by different societies for their fêtes, which sometimes

last several days. No admittance fee is charged, and the place is crowded with booths, where manufactured or real curiosities are exhibited, places where one may shoot at a mark, or listen to a concert. Strolling bands of two or more musicians, armed with violins, guitars, or bagpipes, mingle with the crowd and, stopping wherever they see a group of young people, soon have a circle about them dancing a sort of waltz upon the uneven turf. But the great attraction was always *carne con cuero*, or beef roasted with the hide on ; not a whole animal, but parts of it. Placed on long iron spits before the fires—which were built all about—would be pieces of beef with the hide side next the fire, the whole being delightfully flavored by the smoke from the burning hair and frizzling hide. The odor was always sufficient to fill me with disgust, yet it was very popular, sometimes even being served in the hotel.

XIV.

A BULL FIGHT IN MONTEVIDEO.

BULLS THAT SHOWED FIGHT AND BULLS THAT DID NOT—
SOME CRUEL SCENES—A DISORDERLY ENDING.

I WAS one of a party who were breakfasting one Sunday
at the home of a resident American, when he proposed a visit
to the bull-ring, to show his countrywomen the glories and
horrors of a fight. Our church here is closed for the present,
waiting the arrival of a minister from England; hence our
religion was at a low ebb, and we accepted his invitation.

We rode for half an hour over as bad pavements as any
city in the world can show, the drivers going at the usual
pace of about forty miles to the hour. However, we finally
arrived at the suburban village of La Union, were whirled up
to the outside of the large brick bull-ring, and tried to shake
off some of the dust, while our escort joined a shouting,
surging crowd that was besieging a large grated window, over
which was the sign, " *Boletes de primera clase* "—first class

tickets. Soon he returned, and we entered a low arched passage, climbed a flight of stairs, passed part way around the circle, and, descending as near the arena as we could, seated ourselves on some nice, freshly whitewashed seats.

The building in which we found ourselves is a large brick amphitheatre, with a broad walk on top, which is partly covered by a row of boxes with six seats in each and corrugated iron roofs. Below these in unbroken circles are low brick seats, capable of holding 10,000 people and occupied by about 5,000 on this day. Those on the shady side were the first-class places and some had whitewashed seats on them, while others had movable cushions, each man being handed one as he came in. Below these seats were the entrances and exits for the espadas, banderilleros, picadores, and bulls. Just below the box of the president of the sports was the entrance for the men, and opposite, that for the bulls. There were two circles, a large sanded one in the centre, with a strong board fence some nine feet high surrounding it and several bits of fence placed here and there, just in front of the main one and close to it, for the men to hide behind when too closely pressed. The outer circle was about fifteen feet wide, and this was partitioned off with swinging doors and movable fences. The programme promised us six bulls, two of them imported from Spain, from the flock of his Excellency the Duke of Veragua, and four native animals, besides, four native bulls held in reserve. The Spanish bulls were named Serenity and Vinegar, and did not belie their names. There were four espadas, the first named Joaquin Sanz of Valencia, and the second Juan Gimenez of Ecija. There were three picadores and seven banderilleros, all Spaniards. The prices were $10 for a box, $1 for a seat, $1.50 entrance fee for a first-class adult, and 70 cents for a child. The entrance to the second-class, or sunny seats, was $1 for all ages. At the bottom of the programme were ten announcements by the management: (1.) To avoid crowding at the entrances, the doors will be opened at one o'clock and will close half an hour after the finish, except in case of rainy weather, when the audience will be allowed to remain longer if they wish. (2.) No more bulls will be fought than the programme announces. (3.) No one will be allowed to throw articles into the arena, which might injure the combatants, and no obscene language will be tolerated. (4.) No one but employees will be allowed between the barriers. (5.) Banderillas of fire will be used for every bull who refuses three times to face the picadores. (6.) In case one, two, or all the picadores are injured, the management will not be obliged to furnish others. (7.) Bulls which, in judgment of the president, will not fight, will be led off by the bell-ox. (8). The president will be a person chosen by the management. (9.) If the performance is interrupted by

some unforeseen circumstance, the entrance money will not
be refunded. (10.) Any one who creates a disturbance will
be handed over to the police.

As we took our seats the band was playing a waltz; three
mounted picadores, dressed in yellow, with broad-brimmed gray
felt hats and long steel-pointed rods in their hands, were sta-
tioned around the circle, equidistant, facing the center. Their
horses were sorry-looking nags, and two of them were blind-
folded. Behind each picador stood a man in a jockey suit of
red and yellow, carrying in his hand a cruel rawhide whip to
urge the horse with in case it showed a faint heart or refused
to return to the attack after being wounded. In front of the
President's box stood the banderilleros in the gorgeous, beautiful dress of the bull-fighter; their breeches and jackets a glittering mass of gold and silver, the broad-rimmed black hats with
pompons and loops, the braid of hair down their backs ornamented with the peculiar chignon-like article which they
affect; brilliant-colored silk stockings and low shoes completing
the dress. Alert, graceful, and composed, they stood with
their eyes fixed on the opposite entrance, their red cloaks held
trailing on the ground before them. The door swung slowly
open, and out stepped a fine native bull. For a second he
looked about him astonished, then, catching sight of the red
cloaks, he dashed across the arena, to be met by one of them
being thrown over his head as the banderillero who held it

vaulted to one side, and snatching his cloak towards him, moved, shaking it, to one side. The bull turned to charge for him again, when his eye was caught by a picador on a gray horse. The picador saw him and received him with a stab on his neck from the point of his lance, but the charge was too impetuous, and the picador was unhorsed, while the poor horse received the horns of the bull full in his chest; there was a gush of blood and he rolled over just as a banderillero turned the bull's attention with his red cloak and coaxed him to the other side of the arena, where he and his associates kept him occupied, charging first one cloak and then another until the picador was lifted up and taken out of the ring, and the horse was flogged until he half rose and was dragged into the outer circle. The bull wounded two other horses, and as one of the banderilleros was dazzling him with his cloak he slipped and fell. The bull charged for him, but the man lay as if dead and the bull evidently thought him so, for he charged over him, only tearing his breeches, to attack another who came to his rescue. It was a thrilling moment, and the people, getting excited, began to call for the banderillas. A trumpet sounded from the presidential box, a door swung open, and the picadores vanished, while half of the banderilleros threw aside their cloaks and each of them took two banderillas and prepared to use them. These are wooden sticks about three feet long, wound with colored strips of paper, and in one end having a barbed iron-point. A man would take one in each hand, and standing before the bull, invite an attack by holding them up and waving them. The bull charges and the man, while retreating, reaches over the horns and plants the barbs in the neck, jumping aside at the same instant. The long sticks hang and drag on the wound, irritating the bull tremendously.

The people evidently intended to manage the affair, and the president seemed to occupy the place of an umpire at a base-ball game in their estimation; first they called for the banderillas, and now, when six had been inserted, they began to call for the espada. The audience was almost entirely composed of men of the better class, and they were very noisy, using all sorts of instruments to assist their voices; a man just behind me had a huge cow-bell, which he rang in and out of season, while a crippled Spaniard, who was carried in a man's arms and sat just in front of me, had a splendid pair of lungs, and enjoyed abusing the whole thing immensely; it was not bloody enough for him, and he assured the president, among other things, that cholera was unnecessary this year; the country was already sufficiently disgraced by such a bull-fight. At last the trumpet sounded a few notes, and the espada, with his bright red cloak and glittering sword, entered the arena and bowed and smiled to the audience. A little more torture of the bull, and the espada succeeded in burying his sword up to the hilt, just back of the neck, always attacking him from the front. It was a bad stroke and did not kill, so there was more charging and waving of cloaks until the espada succeeded in pulling the sword out. Then another attack, and again the blade was buried and the stroke a bad one. The sword was pulled out again and found to be broken, but still the espada fought with it until the bull was on his knees, when some one handed him a short, heavy weapon, one blow from which was given between the horns, and the bull rolled over dead. It was such butchery that there was no applause, and the men left the arena in silence, while three caparisoned mules came dashing in, were attached to the carcass, and dashed out with it while the music played.

The second bull refused to fight, turning from the picadores and even from the cloaks of the banderilleros. The populace demanded, "*Fuego! banderillas de fuego! fuego, Señor Presidente!*" But the president declined, and the doors on one side opened to admit two large dun-colored oxen with big bells on their necks. The bull seemed to know them. He joined them, and the three were whipped out of the ring. This was the imported bull named Serenity. The third bull came dashing into the ring with a fresh wound on one of his hind-quarters, given evidently just as he left the stable. To improve his courage, and as he came on in his

8

charge, a banderillero, taking a long pole in his hand, rushed towards him and vaulted clear over him. His fury was short-lived, however, and he soon was condemned by the people, who shouted, "*Fuera! fuera!*" until he was led off. The fourth and fifth bulls were like him, and by this time the populace were getting rather unruly, so the sixth animal was forced to fight. The picadores stuck him until the blood ran in streams down his neck, then six banderillas were planted in his neck; after which the poor wretch tried to escape, and climbed the nine-foot fence four times, only to be driven from one enclosure into another, and finally back into the ring. At last another espada entered, and the fourth time the sword was driven in up to the hilt, the beast fell dead, and was dragged off to the sound of more music. The seventh, eighth, and ninth bulls refused to fight, and were hissed off, the people getting more and more excited, until most of them were on their feet express-ing their sentiments. The other ladies of the party had retired, and I seemed to excite the admiration of the men by having staid, and they were careful to stand on one side so that I could see, and there were no coarse remarks made near me.

The tenth bull was the Spanish Vinegar, and he fought well; in less than ten minutes he had killed three horses and wounded three, in spite of the efforts of the picadores. One he gored to

death in the ring, fighting him until he ceased even to raise his
head; another ran around with his bowels hanging from a wound
until he came to a gate which was opened, and he ran in; the
other was dragged out on his knees; the three wounded ones
pranced out, and then the bull attacked the men, and the people settled down in their seats. There were many narrow escapes,
much vaulting over the fence and jumping behind screens; eight
banderillas were planted, and then the espada came out and
literally butchered him, striking over and over again before he
fell. His carcass was dragged out, and also that of the dead
horse. Once more the picadores took their places, and a tame
bull walked in. This was too much for the audience, and there
was a perfect shower of cushions and seats thrown into the arena,
and the people rose and began to surge to and fro. I sat still
until a man said to my escort: "Get higher up; here come the
chairs and boxes." Then we began to make our way out, and it
was decidedly dangerous, as the people were tearing the boxes
to pieces and hurling everything they could into the arena—
doors, boards, and all. It was slow work getting out, but every
one helped me, all pushing and saying, "*Una señora! cuidado à
la señora!*" As we went out I looked back and saw a wonderful picture. Horses, picadores, banderilleros, and the assistants,
all had retreated to the further side of the circle, and stood there
in their beautiful attire looking up at the enraged multitude and
the missiles hurled at them. On the nearer side stood the bull,

he too gazing up, transfixed with astonishment; and all about me was the surging mobs, the sound of their exclamations and the cracking of breaking timbers filling the air. The few police inside were powerless, but as I came out a company of them armed with rifles filed in, and as we drove away in our carriage the rattle of musketry was the last sound to reach us from the bull ring. It was a horrible three hours that I had passed, and the nervous strain was great. The blood, the butchery of the bulls, the poor wounded horses, goaded on again and again to resist the attack, the quick catching of the breath as a man saved his life by a sudden dexterous twist of his body or leap over the fence, the enthusiasm which animated you in spite of the horror of it, were all trying; yet I am glad I went, for I firmly believe that the world is always better to-day than it was yesterday, and this is but another proof of it; for bull-fighting, which, with all its attendant horrors, was once a favorite and common pastime, has now almost vanished off the face of the earth, and soon we shall know it only from books, as we know of the Inquisition and of slaves sold in the market-place.

XV.

CITY OF BUENOS AYRES.

SCENES ON THE WATER FRONT—A POPULOUS TOWN WITH NAR-
ROW STREETS—THE PLAZA VICTORIA—NOTABLE BUILD-
INGS—THE CATHEDRAL, EXCHANGE, PALACE—POINTS OF
INTEREST.

THERE is a line of steamers plying between Montevideo and
Buenos Ayres whose managers buy up all opposition and manage things to suit themselves. The steamers are fairly good,
and make the trip across the river in about twelve hours, but
one has to take a small boat to, and then scramble over the side
when in Montevideo; and as to getting ashore in Buenos Ayres
before the time when steamers entered the Boca—well! it was a
disagreeable picnic.

Buenos Ayres may be said not to have a harbor, as vessels of
deep draught have to anchor some twelve miles off. There they
discharge their cargo into lighters, which, being flat-bottomed,
can go within half a mile of the shore. From the lighters the

boxes and bales are piled into carts that are drawn by three or more horses, and driven out into the water to reach the lighters until just the backs and heads of the horses are above the water. Immense loads are put into the carts, and the poor horses are soon killed by their work, for not only are their loads heavy, and standing in the water—often very cold—injurious, but they are badly shod, harnessed, and most cruelly beaten as they stagger ashore and strain up the short, steep, illy-paved street which leads to the custom-house. Vessels that draw no more than ten feet can come within four miles of the city, and from their decks the city shows as a long line of buildings stretched along the horizon. Passengers were put into small boats, and, if the river were high enough, rowed to one end of a long pier opposite the custom-house. If the tide was out they went ashore in a cart, like the merchandise, making a most annoying and expensive journey, as every change costs enormously. A port is being built, but it will take a long time to complete it. Work was begun about two miles south of the city and near the original settlement, where a small stream called the Riachuelo empties into the Plate. The Riachuelo was dug out, deepened, and widened, and an embankment built on either side of this basin, with wharves on top of the embankment. A canal-like entrance was excavated as far as the outer harbor, so now a certain number of vessels of deep draught can enter this basin and discharge at the wharves. They would sometimes crowd as many as four hundred in, and it does very well in winter; but the Riachuelo is too small to keep a current flowing through the basin. Thus the water is stagnant, and in summer it makes the air so foul that there is much sickness among the shipping.

This port and the village about it is called the Boca, and it is connected with the city by steam and street cars. The plan of the port is to build a series of basins along the present city front, and a wall-way outside of them, where the river is deep, and then fill between the wall and the basins. This will give them acres and acres of ground, and they sold them long in advance at very high prices.

Buenos Ayres is the capital of the Argentine Republic, not the Argentine Confederation. It used to be the latter, but they have had the war, and the blood has been spilt which seems necessary to weld nations together, and now they are firmly united. Driven to desperation by the tyrannies of Juan Manuel Rosas, a union was formed which triumphed, and in driving him forth as an exile they for a time, at least, drove forth the lawless spirit that reveled in bloody revolutions, and since then the nation has flourished until the late financial troubles. Rosas' life would have paid the forfeit of his years of crime had not the English minister, a man whom he had wantonly insulted, lent the folds of the English flag to protect him, while he and his boxes of treasure were conveyed on board an English merchantman lying in the outer roads.

The city was founded just to the south of the present site—near the Boca—by Pedro del Mendoza, in 1535, and now contains about half a million inhabitants. It is a beautiful city, as a whole, with an amount of business in the streets that crowds them, but the streets are narrow. I am told they were built so because they are so much cooler in summer, but I fancy they were originally built so for purposes of defense as well as coolness.

We landed at the long wharf and found it well filled with Italian emigrants in the picturesque costumes of their native land. Walking up, our attention was called to the line of washerwomen along the shore. They were pursuing the same process as those on the oriental bank of the river, only here the river so seldom rises that the pools of water along the bank are seldom overflowed, and women were washing in pools that were not only white with soap, but some were covered with a green slime. It is not pleasant to contemplate wearing such clothes, and we always tried for a washerwoman who used the water from her cistern, or, as a Japanese boy put it, got water on a string.

At the shore end of the wharf, a long, narrow park extends for quite a distance along the water front, and it is very pretty, with its green grass, trees, and neatly kept walks. The plaza Victoria, named in honor of the victory of the 25th of May, 1810, is only two blocks from the landing, and is the oldest as

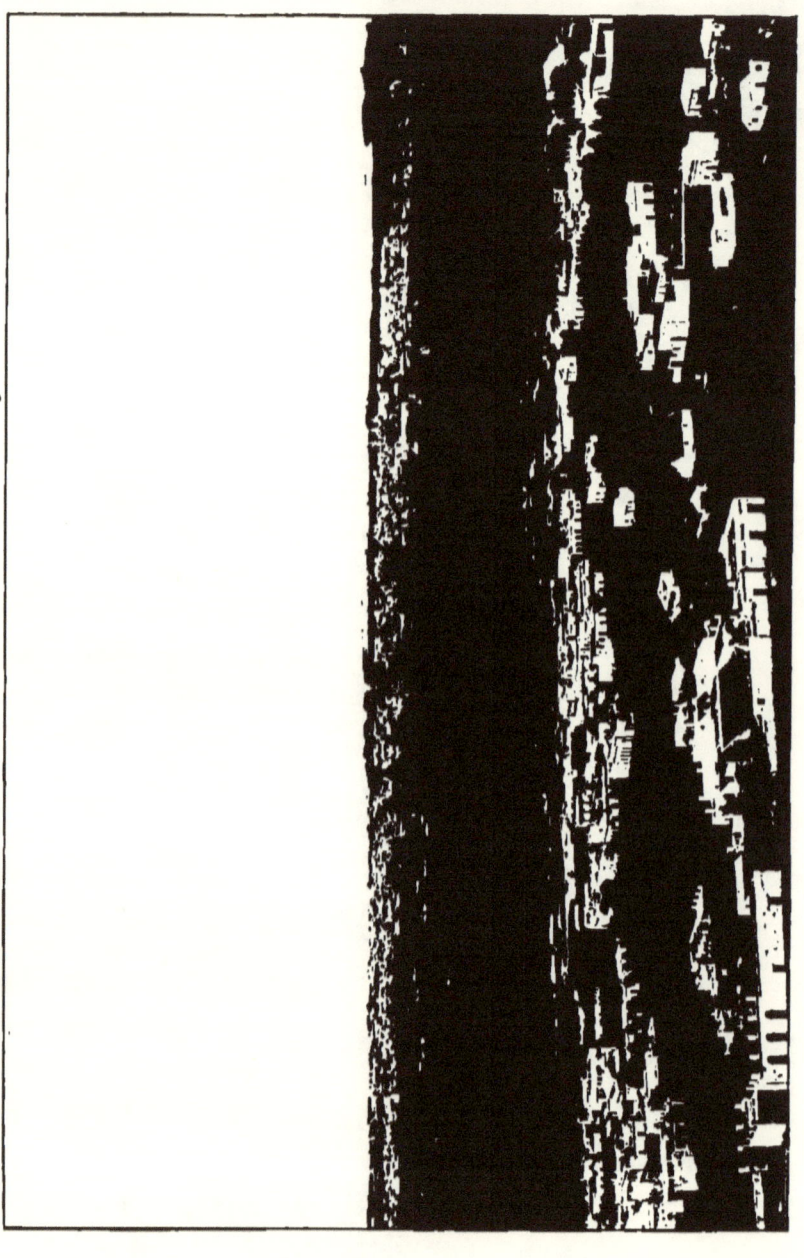

MONTEVIDEO, FROM THE CERRO.

well as the most interesting one in town. It is eight acres in extent, and has two grass plots, intersected by walks and separated by a broad paved roadway. In the center of one plot is an adobe monument to Liberty in a bad state of repair, the adobe peeling off the brick foundation in many places. Gas-pipes outline it so that it may be illuminated, and it is surrounded by an iron railing. In the other plot of grass is a large equestrian bronze statue in honor of Gen. San Martin, I was told, but there is no name on it. He evidently is superior to the traditionary hero, who needs but the naming of his name, the telling of his story.

All around the outside of these inner squares is a double row of royal palms that flourish fairly well in spite of the cold. Then comes the surrounding street, and finally the buildings. One of these standing on a corner is the Cathedral, a large imposing white building, with a fine portico. There are no towers, and the dome is so far back that one does not see it well from the street level. Passing the portico, you enter, to find a building which impresses you by its great size and the simple decorations in white and gold, even the altars being chiefly noticeable for the falls of gold and silver lace that decorate them. Leo XIII., the present Pope, was attached to the cathedral when a young priest, and is said to have officiated at its altars.

A chapel off the right aisle contained the remains of the great general, San Martin, which are inclosed in a splendid tomb standing in the center of the chapel, an inscription claiming him as the liberator of the Argentine, Chilian, and Peruvian republics. The Roman Catholic religion is supported by the government and flourishes financially in consequence. Next the Cathedral is the large episcopal residence, and on the same side of the plaza, nearer the river, is the splendid new Exchange, the old building being cleverly incorporated by the architect.

The whole side of the plaza next the river is occupied by a government building that I generally heard spoken of as the Palace. It is two stories and a mansard roof in height, and has two grand entrances. It is guarded day and night by soldiers with fixed bayonets, and here are the offices of the President, his cabinet, and many other government officials of minor importance. It is not yet finished, a terrace at one end and the part facing the river being only about half completed.

One of the custom-house buildings is next, and just across Balcarce Street is the low building with a big entrance which contains the House of Parliament; there being only one hall, the senators and representatives sitting on alternate days. I wished much to enter, but was informed that my sex debarred me, and all the satisfaction I could get out of it was to ask every Argentine I was introduced to, why? and then let him explain until he got tired. It was at the door of this building that an attempt was made to assassinate General Roca when he was President.

Our minister, Bayliss W. Hanna, was the first to reach the wounded man and give him protection and assistance, an act which was never forgotten by the Argentine government, and Mr. Hanna is a prominent figure in the painting, which was executed by Señor Blanes, the distinguished Uruguayan artist, upon the order of Gen. Roca, in commendation of the event. It represents the senate in session, President Roca present with a bloody bandage about his head and Minister Hanna standing in a small box, one or two other diplomats showing behind him.

XVI.

SHOPS OF BUENOS AYRES.

PONCHOS IN VARIOUS STYLES—VALUABLE RUGS AND ROBES—
FINE PARAGUAYAN FABRICS—BOMBILLAS AND MATE CUP
—HABIT OF MATE-DRINKING.

THE streets of Buenos Ayres are uncommonly narrow, and
the sidewalks are made to match. Two persons can pass, but
that is all, and the men are very rude about stopping to talk in
groups, which entirely obstruct the sidewalk. And they do
not move unless you deliberately halt and request them to let
you by. Then they do so with smiles and bows, to show their
perfect willingness to oblige. Some of the shops are filled
with beautiful objects of art, generally from France or Italy;
but as a rule the windows are small and low, not calculated for
a fine display of goods. The majority seemed filled with
gentlemen's wearing apparel, such a charming display of dainty
underwear, and the men one meets are so well-dressed, so
altogether pleasing to the eye that even a stranger must con-

done their getting in your way, and their other habit of remark-
ing in audible tones upon your appearance, telling you frankly
if you look well or ill, if your bonnet and gown are becoming
or not; letting you know, in short, how you appear to a
stranger. It makes me smile even now to remember the indig-
nation of a gentleman from one of our Southern States because
the loungers on Calle Florida informed the lady he was
escorting that she was decidedly homely.

Calle Florida is the Broadway of the city and is thronged
every afternoon, the largest crowds being near the cafés. The
women wear Parisian gowns and hats, and when young are as
pretty, plump little pigeons as one could desire. Now and
then a beautiful elderly woman passes; the majority, however,
lose all shape as they age. There are a great many large
wholesale stores filled with samples and boxes, chiefly English
and German goods, which make their way by railroad and ox
team into the interior. The Buenos Ayres papers always give
the amount of skins and country produce brought into the city
daily, and among the reports was one market where everything
quoted was brought in in large prairie-schooner wagons drawn
by numbers of patient oxen.

The streets are filled with carts loaded with merchandise and
drawn by several horses, the leaders being harnessed with such
long traces that they often meander all over the sidewalk,
being quite beyond the control of the driver, and one has con-

stantly to keep an eye on passing vehicles to look out for horses coming in one's way. The Argentine is fond of good horseflesh, and there are many fine specimens to be seen drawing beautiful carriages, especially in the afternoon in Palermo Park.

A very interesting store to me was one filled with the products of the country. There was wine from the province of San Juan, Mendoza, Rioja, and Catamarca, both red and white, and some of the claret from Catamarca was quite good. There were piles and piles of ponchos, made of vicuña, llama, alpaca, and sheep's wool. The finest and most expensive were of vicuña. One beauty as soft and fine as silk cost $1,000. The cheapest and coarsest are of sheep's wool and bring from $3 to $4 each. They are all woven by hand and wear wonderfully well, the fine vicuña ones often being heirlooms. I was told that instead of putting a chip on his shoulder or requesting some one to tread on the tail of his coat, that the man who wears the poncho when seeking for a fight holds one corner over his shoulder, allowing the other to trail on the ground, and thus parades until he meets a kindred spirit, who picks up the glove by treading on the trailing corner, and then the fight begins. The color is generally some shade of brown, from the lightest *café au lait* to a dark chocolate, except, of course, the alpacas, and, being natural colors, wear out before they fade, the hair from the neck and stomach giving one shade, that on the back another, and so on. The pattern is universally stripes, running lengthwise. The markets are now flooded with imitations made in England, and as they are of good wool, as well as cheaper, of course, than the handmade, they are worn a great deal, but they are a different looking article from the native ones, even when as thin and fine. There are heavy saddle-bags and saddle-cloths of woolen and a good many jams and marmalades made in the northern provinces where fruit is plentiful.

Another, to me, fascinating store was filled with rugs made from the skins of native animals, and there were also large piles of the raw material so that one could select the skins and have a rug made to order. The prettiest, as well as the most fragile, are those made from the native ostrich and costing about $50 each. Next come those made from the necks of the vicuña, which are from $80 to $130 each; they are fawn and white in color, and the hair is as soft as down. There are guanaco robes from $15 to $40, and grebe, fox, otter, and other skins for all sorts of prices. Two other stores were charming, and their contents beguiling, although hidden away on side streets and hard to find. They were for the sale of Paraguayan articles, among which is lace that looks like spider webs, and is called so (ñanduti) in the Guarani tongue, made by the native women, who were taught by the Jesuit missionaries many years ago; gold puzzle rings made of fine wires fitted together to make a broad band; bows and arrows, necklaces of guanaco toe-nails and of monkey's teeth; specimens of rude pottery and bales of maté leaves, covered with skins, the hair on the outside; bombillas, a tube with a bulb at one end, and the bulb pierced with tiny holes to strain the maté herb from the tea as it is sucked up, and a seemingly endless variety of maté cups. Some of these latter were made of silver, but generally they are small gourds, with a piece of the stem left on for a handle. Some are allowed to retain their natural color, others are dyed red and a pattern engraved upon them, but the majority are dyed black and left plain. The carving on some is very elaborate. Some are mounted on stands of silver, and elaborately bound and decorated with the same precious metal. Occasionally the fruit is tied while growing and made to assume all sorts of shapes. A small round hole is cut in one side to clean out the seeds, and also for the introduction of the bombilla. These bombillas are generally made of silver or tin, but I secured a few of Indian make, bamboo tube with basket-work bulbs, and in Cordoba we got from the nuns some dainty ones of decorated bamboo tubes and white horsehair strainers.

Maté, generally called Paraguayan tea, is made from the leaf of a small tree of the holly species—*ilex Paraguayensis*—which flourishes in parts of Paraguay. The leaves are gathered, prepared, and then carefully packed in fresh hide bags, which contract when drying and make a package as hard as a stone. It

is a yellowish green in color, and a teaspoonful of maté powder
is put into the gourd, a small lump of sugar also if you like it,
and then the cup is filled with boiling water, the bombilla inserted, and the infusion sucked through it.   Fully three-fourths
of the natives of Uruguay and the Argentine drink maté, and
the quantity they consume is astonishing.   A silversmith in the
town of Paysandu told me he only drank thirty to fifty cups in
a day, and I have often seen a dozen emptied one after the
other, and the cup sent out for more.   Officers and soldiers
standing at the barrack doors are drinking maté, and there is
generally a gourd passing among the guard at the palace.
Women and girls run to the door to see something pass, or
stand there talking, with the inevitable maté gourd in one hand.
In small stores a man will imbibe maté while attending to your
wants.   In short, you see it used everywhere except in the
houses of fashionable people in the cities, where it is no longer
stylish to drink it, tea having taken its place.   I have often
tasted it, as it is the universal custom to offer some refreshment
to callers, and when maté was passed of course we partook.   It
tastes like weak green tea, and would not be disagreeable were
it not that in a group of people only one gourd and one bombilla
is used, being passed to each person in turn, and one has to put
in their mouth the unwiped end of a metal tube that has been
in more or less mouths present.

There are several markets about town, and they are always

well filled. Vegetables are plenty, but expensive; meat cheap and poor. It does not seem to have been properly bled, and is very lean. It is also sold too soon after being killed. In the morning there are plenty of fish, which are brought from Montevideo. Fruit is scarce, and, like everything else, expensive.

XVII.

OBJECTS OF INTEREST IN THE SUBURBS OF BUENOS AYRES.

CURIOUS BURIAL CUSTOMS — THE NAVAL ACADEMY — THE PUBLIC SCHOOLS AND THEIR AMERICAN TEACHERS — PALERMO PARK AND ZOOLOGICAL GARDEN.

THERE is an old, aristocratic burial-ground in Buenos Ayres, which is called Recoleta, and within its boundaries rests the dust of Lavalle, Brown, and Alvear, with many another of their famous generals, admirals, and Brazilian patriots. It is quite at one side of the city, and was doubtless entirely in the country when first consecrated, but now the broad new avenues reach out to it, and only the large park, which begins just here, keeps it from being surrounded by bricks and mortar other than of its own choosing, for a high brick wall shuts it in from the traffic of the street, and a high, wide gate of iron bars forms the only entrance. Inside, and to the left of the gate, is an office, in which sits a clerk behind a table waiting for customers. On the right is a bare, cheerless little chapel, with an altar, before which stood the two

black carpenter's horses to rest a coffin on.   A priest in his long
black cassock sat reading a book with a most demure and
proper-looking cover, so I fancy it was a book of prayers.   Everything appeared so ready, all was so prepared, that one involuntarily looked out into the street to see if a funeral procession
was not approaching.   Passing on, the visitor enters a labyrinth
of narrow walks—for here space means money—on either side
of which are tombs and monuments of every conceivable size,
shape, and design.   Different colored stones are used, and occasionally a full-length statue varies the monotony.   Some are
cheap and tawdry, others, and by far the greater number, beautiful.   The favorite plan seemed to be to buy a plot, about eight
or more feet square, build over it the prettiest chapel of marble
one can afford, excavate the earth a long way down like a square
well, concrete this, and fasten strong iron brackets into the wall
on each side every few feet, these brackets serving to hold the
coffins.   An altar is built in the chapel, and in front of it, in
the floor, is an open grating, which is raised to admit the coffins,
and through which they can be plainly seen.   In some of the
oldest ones the vault below is full, and coffins have been placed
on brackets about the chapel walls.   The entrance to nearly all
the chapel tombs is an iron grated gate with glass doors inside,
the glass doors being always set ajar or left wide open for ventilation.   One imagines all sorts of odors, and as all sorts of diseases are buried there it is to be hoped that the coffins are

hermetically sealed. There are many wreaths of flowers on coffins and in the chapels ; some made of immortelles, others of beads, but the majority of natural beauties. There are fountains and evergreen trees to brighten things up, while about some of the very oldest graves there is a bit of bright green turf, the body having been laid at rest in Mother Earth in the usual way —a flat slab on top, and around it all an iron railing.

On one side of the grave-yard stands the poor-house, a large handsome building, with a lovely garden full of flowers about it. I always wonder when I see such beautiful things about charitable institutions if the poor inmates are allowed to enjoy them, or if they are for show. As I said before, just here begins the park, called Recoleta, after the cemetery. It is long, narrow, well laid out, and pleasing. Perhaps a little too much imitation petrified wood, which makes bridges, lies about like fallen trunks for benches, and forms a grotto, and appears everywhere, but the grass is so green, the trees, flowers, shrubs, and running water so pretty, that one is charmed with the place.

At the foot of the grotto is a pond with lovely ducks of varied plumage swimming about in it, and, just beyond, benches whence one sees out into the yellow expanse of river water, with ships passing to and fro; there is a nice carriage drive throughout its whole length, which in the afternoon is thronged with fine turnouts.

Near the southern end, on the Avenida Alvear, was the naval school, modeled somewhat after ours, by Gen. Domingo Sarmiento, who represented his country at Washington for a while, admired many of our institutions immensely, and later, when he was President, introduced many of them to his own people.

The naval academy has lately been moved more than 200 miles up the Parana River to a place which, when compared to the Avenida Alvear, is a howling wilderness. Our public schools were especially interesting to Gen. Sarmiento, and he brought out teachers from the States to preside over them, and as the system spreads a few more are added every year. They are well paid and looked after, being under the protection of the government; but the standard is high, only the best are taken, and the work is hard, besides the fact that to accept a position means living here away from one's friends and country. Teaching is carried on principally in Spanish. English is only a branch, so the teachers must speak the language like natives. ˙ They are a fine body of women, and we met some charming ones. The first ones married so soon after their arrival that the government began to be discouraged, and they are still in demand; for the *rara avis*, a woman who can make her own living, order her life and household so that, although she live alone, not a breath of scandal touches her, is admired and desired, yet it is difficult for the people to believe their daughters could do the same. Occasionally the government shows its appreciation of their work in a manner that must be gratifying. For instance, the Roman Catholic is the established church, yet when the Papal legate interfered unwarrantably with the management of a school under a Miss Armstrong, and both appealed to headquarters, he was given twenty-four hours to leave the country in, and left. This is the story as I several times heard it related, and the sister of the young woman afterward told me, at my request, the tale, and it did not differ materially. Passing along the streets in the afternoon you see children pouring out of the graded school buildings even as they do at home, and it warms your heart to see them and think what strides this country will make once these children come of age, the boys to force free votes and a true republic, the girls to aid them by making them intelligent companions and forming in their nurseries the minds and manners of their children. They use the kindergarten as well as the graded and normal systems. In small villages there is always a school, and while I have heard foreigners speak slightingly of these outposts, they always struck me as quite as good as any I saw in Germany, better, in fact, because they are free.

The large city park is called Palermo, and lies in one of the suburbs, its official name being, I believe, Third of February, but as it is never called so it does not count. It is reached

by carriage, horse-cars, or the Tigre railroad. We went out
the second way, taking a train at the Plaza Victoria, which,
after passing through the city and way out into the suburbs,
stopped before a large gateway, inside of which another car
was waiting to take passengers to the military school which
is in the grounds. We entered and had a regular John
Gilpin ride for about fifteen minutes.

There was a track to run on, but the driver preferred the
pavement, so we rattled and jounced, the windows rattled and
shook, while one of the male passengers tried to hold the floor-
grating in place, which task kept him busy. The end of the
route was reached with all our teeth in our heads, but we had
not enjoyed the scenery. We saw the low, white buildings of
the military school at one side and walked on past it into the
grove of trees and along the neat gravel paths. There are
about fifty acres in all, perfectly flat, with trees and flowers
planted in numbers, and the former chiefly eucalyptus, the only
notable exception being the rows of palms beside the main
drive.

There is an extensive zoological garden with many good
specimens of lamas, condors, monkeys, leopards, and any
quantity of ducks, as well as a pen and tank filled with carpinchos, an animal that looks to me like a cross between a pig
and an otter. They live along the banks of rivers in this
country, spending a great deal of time in the water, and are

INDEPENDENCE SQUARE. MONTEVIDEO

killed and eaten by the natives, the flesh of the young ones being said to taste like pork. They have the shortest kind of a tail, waddle when walking, and are covered with brownish gray bristles.

A stream of water is led about through the park, and, in addition to the ducks which live in the ponds, many wild ones alight daily to feed. Pretty little bridges cross the stream, and there are seats and pavilions all about. A band plays on Thursday and Sunday afternoons, when the grand drive is sure to be crowded with handsome carriages filled with the fashionables of the city, and drawn by splendid horses, most of them imported. This park was another of Sarmiento's ideas.

XVIII.

THE CITY OF LA PLATA.

ITS SPLENDID BANKS, MUSEUM, PARK, AND PUBLIC BUILDINGS—
HOW IT WAS PROPOSED TO MAKE A SEAPORT OUT OF AN
INLAND VILLAGE—GREAT CALCULATIONS ON THE FUTURE—
SUBURBS OF BELGRANO AND TIGRE.

THERE are a great many large plazas in Buenos Ayres and
most of them well cared for. The city spreads out over an
immense amount of ground, thanks to the one-storied houses,
and in riding about on the various street-car lines one is often
surprised by pretty plazas, and also surprised by the lack of
knowledge as to their names and extent on the part of the
other people in the car. They are all willing and almost
anxious to discuss the question and help you, but they cannot.
Victoria I have already attempted to describe. San Martin, at
the northern end of Florida Street, has a colossal statue in
bronze of Gen. San Martin on horseback, and a great many
lovely flowers, as well as odd-looking trees and shrubs. It is

surrounded by a wide avenue, and here, in the afternoon, troops from the neighboring barracks come out to drill, the dark, swarthy faces of the men, who seem mostly Indians and negroes, the white faces of the officers, the full, baggy breeches of the men, and the strange music of the band, all being very attractive. As they moved, the undulating lines reminded me strongly of the Italian Bersaglieri, but the step is different— one foot seems put down with more force than the other. They seemed well-armed and equipped, but must have been inefficiently or badly drilled, keeping front badly and failing in detail.

Plaza Constitucion is unusually large, and here there are always a greater or less number of large country bullock-carts, like our old prairie wagons, only these have much larger wheels so as to lift the body higher out of the mud, and the majority have only two wheels. Blue seems to be the favorite color to paint the wagon bodies, and the roof, instead of being even with the ends of the body, projects slightly before and behind. They are drawn by from three to six yoke of large oxen, with the cruel way of fastening them that is prevalent in these countries. Instead of a yoke they take a heavy beam of wood, lay it just behind the horns of the two animals, tie the horns firmly to the end and lash the center to the pole, so they draw entirely by their horns. The weight brings their heads about down to their knees, and their starting eyeballs and the expression on their poor faces show they are in torture. Finally I declined to look at them in their trouble and looked away when I saw a cart coming. The drivers are generally men from the interior, and they bring in cattle and nutria skins and all sorts of country produce.

There is a large number of newspapers published in the city, and there is a beautiful illustrated paper also, but none of their dailies pleased me as much as *El Siglo*, of Montevideo, which was most ably edited. The news came high, as papers were dear, but they did not copy one another as our papers in the States are apt to do, and you found all the news in their columns. On the Plaza Constitucion is a large railway station, and here, one lovely day, we took a train for the city of La Plata.

When Buenos Ayres was finally chosen as the seat of the general government, the province of Buenos Ayres selected a site, about twenty-five miles to the south, and here in the fields they laid out a city to be called La Plata. The railway to it passes over a flat but fertile plain, with cultivated fields and many houses, and occasionally we halted at thrifty-looking little villages, with the usual number of eucalyptus trees about them. There were birds singing in the hedges, and cattle and native ostriches feeding in the fields. Altogether it was a flat, smiling, prosperous-looking bit of country. Arrived at our destination, we alighted in a large, splendid, almost finished station, built, as is everything else in this city, with two eyes to the future. Millions of money have been spent, and all that now is needed is people to live in the houses and throng the streets. They are coming, but very slowly. The streets are broad, straight, and well-paved, as are also the sidewalks. There are several fine government buildings, and to each is allotted a whole square, the building being set in the center, and the remaining space laid out as a garden, filled with flowers and fountains, so that each building has a lovely setting.

The Banco de la Provincia and the Banco Hipotecario surpass any bank buildings that I ever saw or heard of. They are like palaces. Each one stands in the center of a city square, and, like the government buildings, is several stories high, of gray stone, with fine, grand entrances, and the grounds about them beautifully laid out, with drives, walks, statues, flowers, and shrubs. On the side of the city toward the river, which is nine miles off, a grand park is laid out, and hundreds of eucalyptus trees have been planted and are flourishing, but it needs more care than it gets. In the park is the museum building, and it will be a fine one when completed. There is a curving drive guiding one up to the fine flight of steps below the entrance door, and passing the latter you find yourself in a large, circular hall, ornamented with frescoes, which seemed to me to be horrible daubs, artistically considered, yet they were interesting because they represented scenes from the life of the aborigines. In one, a number of people with fewer clothes than ballet dancers, were cutting up and eating a mammoth turtle; in another they were throwing the lasso, and in the third, these sons of the soil are threading a trackless forest. Two halls were in order, one containing the collection of fossils, for which this museum of the province of Buenos Ayres is famous through all the world, and the other hall showing a fine collection of ancient Peruvian pottery. Passing through the park and keeping on toward the river, one comes to the little village of Ensenada. It is six miles inland, but a grand scheme is on foot to build a system of docks and dikes to make this a river port. A large part of the work is done, and if the money supplies do not give out, it will in time be accomplished. Small trading vessels can now come up as far as Ensenada through a canal, while large ships come alongside the docks several miles down. The work is in charge of Dutchmen, and is being much better done than at Buenos Ayres in the Boca. A railroad to Buenos Ayres leads right down to the entire length of the proposed improvements. The village is now a dusty, dirty, uninteresting little place to the ordinary tourist.

There is a street-railway service in La Plata, and hacks are plenty and cheap. They have gas, electric-lights, and, in short, it is a city of to-day. There are several pretty suburbs to Buenos Ayres, but Belgrano was my favorite; the flowers, trees, and *quintas*—country houses—being especially pretty, while there was also an attractive, sloping park, mostly of green-sward, between the town and railway station, with a nice large ombu tree to sit under, and enjoy the country air and view. The ombu is a native of this part of the world, and belongs to the fig family. It grows to a fine height and the branches give a dense shade, under which no insect cares to dwell. The trunk always looked to me too large in proportion for beauty, but its most striking peculiarity is the big bunch of roots at the base of the trunk showing above the ground.

Tigre is a favorite summer resort with many, and it has numerous waterways about it like canals, which are the southern mouths of the Parana delta. It is pleasant pulling about upon them, the low dividing islands being filled with fruit trees, especially peach and pear. Every here and there a house nestles among the trees, making a pretty picture, or you pass a float and boathouse, all the boat clubs of the city having quarters here. There is also the national navy-yard, and some torpedo-boats and small craft were laid up alongside the bank. It is difficult to imagine how anything of much draft could be gotten out if needed, unless they made a long trip up this branch of the Parana to San Pedro, and then came down the main branch. Tigre gets its name from the capture there of a South American leopard, which the natives call a tiger. It probably came down the river on one of the many floating islands, and must have made a long journey. When we went ashore to explore one of these islands the mosquitoes were so numerous and hungry that we returned to our boat and to Buenos Ayres dinnerless, but having furnished dinner to many hungry hummers.

XIX.

UP THE URUGUAY RIVER—CITY OF COLONIA.

A MEMORABLE CHRISTMAS—THE HEROIC THIRTY-THREE—
WHERE THE FIRST BLOW FOR INDEPENDENCE WAS
STRUCK—THE LIEBIG EXTRACT HEAD-QUARTERS—PICT-
URESQUE COSTUMES.

ON the Uruguay bank of the river of the same name is the ancient and pretty little town of Colonia. It is built on a point stretching out into the river and is near the junction of the Parana and Uruguay, which unite to form the Rio de la Plata—or " The Platte," as Englishmen persist in calling it— some eighty or ninety miles above Montevideo. It was one of the first forts, and was held alternately by the Portuguese and Spanish in colonial days, being a bone of contention because of its situation and the large settlements of Indians near at hand. As seen from the river it looks very gray and quite large, the two more prominent objects being the church with two towers

10

and a round dome and a round windmill that looks as if it had drifted down here from Holland and felt lonely and forlorn.

Christmas day! and a lovelier one never dawned, as far as nature was concerned, than that which greeted us one year not long ago, in the little town of Colonia del Sacramento, which lay smiling in the sunshine; the fair, green country stretched away on either side, and a faint, soft, northern breeze rippled the water, idly flapped the sails of an anchored schooner, and, farther out, lifted the pennant and fluttered the folds of the ensign on one of Uncle Sam's men-of-war that looked as bright as paint and care could make her. At the wharf lay a little passenger steamer that in the morning had come over from Buenos Ayres; about noon she got up steam for the return trip, and soon after, three young men came down the narrow, crooked old street that widened where it reached the police barracks, until there was quite a little plaza between them, the hotel and the head of the wharf. One of the men turned into the police barracks, the other two kept on until they reached a watchman's hut at the shore end of the wharf, behind which they placed themselves and carefully watched the plaza. There were a good many people in the hotel, dining; while a few came straying down the street and went on board the steamer.

Finally, as it was nearing time for the steamer to leave, two men appeared upon the scene. One glanced about rather apprehensively, for he knew that he had ruined the daughter of the Jefe Politico, some two years before and then refused to marry her, taking refuge and marrying in the neighboring republic. Her father followed him to the Argentine at the time, seeking his life, and could not find him, but left word that he must keep out of Uruguay or take the consequences. He had ventured over, because he knew the Jefe was in Montevideo, but he forgot the sons, yet they were there, and, when they saw him coming, advanced, and firing began; for a few minutes the four men were rushing about the open space, then the betrayer fell, and his brother-in-law was chased into a little butcher-shop and finished. Then the firing ceased, and the police sallying out gathered up two dead men, two badly wounded men, four pistols, and a sword cane; but they could not gather up the blood which was in spots all over the pavement, sidewalks, and houses. The people gathered as if by magic, as soon as the firing ceased, for one soon learns to seek shelter in South America, when one hears shots in the street; and then the tumult began. The two wounded boys, eighteen and twenty-four years of age, were behind the barred archway of the police quarters with their brother, who passed in there as they first came down. These boys seem to have been rather wild, and the father was said to be then in Montevideo explaining something they had written; anyway, in spite of the stain on their honor that they had wiped out, they were intensely unpopular, and the people wanted their blood, seeming entirely reckless as to how much of their own was spilt in getting that for which they thirsted.

Uruguay is divided into provinces, and the chief civil officers, who are appointed by the president, and represent him, are called Jefe Politicos, political chiefs, the Constitution providing that they shall not be military men. Under them is a Primero Official, first official, who acts in their absence; hence the first officer took charge in Colonia and proceeded to act. He had only twelve police, and in answer to his telegrams for help sent to Montevideo, he was told to do the best he could. Twelve police to guard two wounded boys and prevent a revolution in the town by calming the excited populace who were collecting in groups, painting red daggers on doors and talking excitedly. The brother-in-law who was murdered because he happened to be with the betrayer, was much liked and numerously related. He had lived in the country, but wishing educational advantages for his eight children, he had just moved into town and opened a small shop, where he lived with his family, as well as the helpless mother of his wife, and his death seemed without excuse. In a couple of hours we saw two cheap coffins carried down the street and taken into the police barracks, soon they were brought out with the bodies in them,

which must have been stripped, as beside each coffin walked
a man with a hat and a bundle of bloody clothes. I was
told that their throats had been cut, and had grown so
used to tales of cutting throats of dead people and prisoners
that I see no reason to doubt it. A crowd followed the
bodies to the little shop where the widow and children were
waiting, and by this time the first officer, who was thoroughly
frightened and longing for help, bethought him of the man-
of-war in the harbor. He appealed to the Captain for armed
men to prevent riot and bloodshed and aid him in protect-
ing his prisoners as well as the lives of innocent people
who would be killed.

He was advised by the Captain not to call for aid unless
he positively needed it, but seeing his position and hearing
the people talk, it was. impossible not to agree as to the
gravity of the situation, and as he insisted, some of our
marines, prepared for business, were put in boats and taken
to the shore, but not allowed to land until the Captain had
once more seen the official, and urged him to make an appeal
the better class of people to aid him and try and do without external assistance.

Finally, he said the men could go back, and that if there
was immediate danger he would make a signal by firing a
gun and hoisting a lantern, then he would need help and
was assured that he should have it. Twilight came and

went, and the stars came out, making a glorious Christmas night, but still the little town was troubled, some three hundred men gathered in a hall and declined to separate or help the First Official, his prisoners were unpopular and he could not get anyone to forego the pleasures of a revolution by helping him to avert it. At last he saw no other course open to him, and at nine o'clock he made the signal for help. All was quiet on the ship, the men were in their hammocks and the officers grouped on deck or in the ward-room, talking of the day ashore ; but in a moment all was activity, the marines jumped into their clothing, and receiving ammution and rations, took their places in the boats that had been manned and brought alongside; fifteen minutes past nine and they shoved off from the ship. Twenty-five men and an officer landed at the wharf, formed and marched through the crowd to the police barracks' gate, turned in and vanished from the following gaze of the crowd, but their appearance, bearing and business air, had been marked, the crowd knew they were there, and it made a nest of hornets that they did not care to disturb, so without any orders or warnings, group after group dissolved and went home, the grand meeting dispersed and all slept but those on guard—so passed the birthday of the Prince of Peace. The next morning the dead men were buried and some violent talk was indulged in over the remains, but the knowledge of an obstinate fight, if a row was begun or the barracks attacked, cooled their ardor effectually, and when in the afternoon a little Uruguayan man-of-war came gliding into port, all was calm on the surface; but soldiers were landed and the place put under martial law, the President having deposed the old Jefe Politico, and contrary to law, having appointed a military man in his place, who came up on the vessel. Our marines returned aboard and peace was gradually restored, but a number of cow-boys and hard characters came into the town the next day in hopes of finding a pretty row on hand from which they could pluck some advantage.

The town now has about 2,000 inhabitants and seems a thriving, happy, quiet place. There are some curious old streets with worn pavements, high side-walks, and crumbling houses, with stone benches along the fronts, on which Spaniards and Portuguese have lounged, feasting their triumphs, and quarreling over defeats before our century was begun. Here the houses are low and set close to the street, the windows and doors uncommonly small and protected by heavy wooden shutters, the interiors dark, smoke-stained, and irregular, contrasting forcibly with the gardens at the rear, full of bright flowers and sunshine.

In the new part of the town the principal streets are General Flores and the Eighteenth of July. These are broad, well paved, and laid out in straight lines, the houses and shops along them shining with fresh paint.   There is a large plaza, carefully graveled, with benches and some tiny trees set around the sides. This is quite a new plaza and arranged in the latest Montevidean fashion, but I liked the little, old grass-grown one beside the church much better.   Just on the outskirts of the village is the bull-ring, and we investigated it thoroughly when empty, but never happened to be there during the season, which is in summer.   Bull fights are not allowed in the Argentine, but they are in Uruguay, so, as Buenos Ayres is only thirty miles away, across the river, some capitalists built the ring at Colonia, run a steamer over for the fights, and thus the native of Argentine can easily satisfy his longings for a bloody fight.

About half a mile beyond was the cemetery, and near that the beach where one can still gather bola stones left there by the Indians, for here was their largest village of all those near the colony.   The views of the surrounding country are lovely, rolling, undulating fields of rich green clover, with cactus hedges and cattle roaming about, seemingly at will; here and there a clump of trees and under them the gleam of the white house of some estanciero.   Then comes the broad river with its many islands, some of the latter forming the harbor, as there is no curve to the shore, only a straight stretch of green bank, which leads you on, up past Martin Garcia flats, which are always bestrewn with wrecks and vessels aground, and so on up the Uruguay river.

The Uruguay is a magnificent river, which rises in Brazil, sweeps around in a colossal curve on its way to the ocean, and so curving forms the western boundary of Uruguay, separating it from the Argentine province of Entre Rios. Broad and deep, with low banks on either side, and some low islands in it, the river is an ideal highway for commerce, but it is not picturesque. Miles of low, marsh-like banks, covered with coarse grass and gnarled, stunted trees, among which live snakes, leopards, and carpinchos; here and there the hut of a wood-gatherer in a tiny clearing, its mud walls and roof of brown thatch seeming to melt into the natural tints of its surroundings until it is scarcely visible; here and there a long stretch of green meadow, a low bluff, or a view of rolling country, relieves the monotony; but always, everywhere, herds of horned cattle, horses, and sheep grazing and wandering about. This is what you see day after day, except the small pretty towns on the banks. Below Paysandu they are all, with one exception, on the Uruguay side of the river, that bank being the highest, and they are generally built on a point that stretches out into the river or on a low bluff. Carmelita is on a point, and next above is Nueva Palmyra, famous as the place near which thirty-and-three Orientales landed and raised the standard of revolt, thus beginning the war which ended in the liberation of their native Uruguay from the yoke of Brazil. The thirty-three are worshipped as heroes, almost as saints, and an old man who sometimes came to the hotel in

Montevideo to play billiards with friends was pointed out to me as most admirable and worthy of note, because he fought under the thirty-three. He had snow-white hair and a fine, intellectual face. The thirty-three made their plans and arrangements in the Argentine province of Entre Rios, and crossing the river, landed on a sandy beach just above Nueva Palmyra. The exact spot is marked by a low, white monument, which is soon to be surrounded by a park, the government having accepted the adjacent land for that purpose. Fray Bentos and Independencia are built on two points with only a curving beach between, Independencia being a regular town and Fray Bentos consisting solely of the great Liebig extract-of-beef factory, buildings dependent on it, and cottages for the workmen. At the wharf lay four large foreign barks and a small Uruguayan steamer, all taking in cargoes.

The highest town we could go to was the large one of Paysandu, and here we stopped for some time. It is built on ground which slopes gradually toward the river, and the houses look like orchestra chairs as viewed from the stage, the stage in this case being the broad river, while at the farther end of the main aisle or street stands the cathedral. Paysandu is a thriving place, with a good deal of commerce in hides, skins, and beef tongues, and is soon to be connected by rail with Montevideo. The firm of merchants doing the most business, and having the only fine large warehouses in the place, is that of Hufnagel & Plottier, the elder member being an American, one of our citizens, and also our vice-consul. The city was a favorite fighting ground during the frequent revolutions that formerly swept over the country, and some brave fighting has been done there, one of its defenses being celebrated in prose and poetry.

The streets are ill-paved, but the sidewalks are good and the houses also, having pretty inner courts and gardens filled with plants and fruit trees. Some of the streets have orange trees planted along the curbs, and they look very pretty with the ripe fruit and flowers on them. The cathedral is a large, fine one, with two towers in front and a dome over the high altar. Its proportions are good, and the interior, with its simple decorations, admirable. On the occasion of our first visit there were several women moving about, pinning large bows of ribbon on the clean white altar-cloths, placing immense bunches of sweet natural flowers everywhere, preparing for Sunday, which was the feast of Our Lady of the Rosary. Several stores are for the sale of fine silver ornaments for saddles and bridles, they being made in Paysandu, the silver hammered into beautiful shapes and designs by the intelligent workmen, the whip handles, knife-sheaths, and saddle-yokes being especially ornate and good. Most of the men dress in the modern *guacho*, or cow-boy style, that is, some kind of a low, soft hat, flannel shirt and *poncho*, a broad belt, pair of very full trousers, plaited in at the waist and around the ankles, the costume finished off by a

pair of low boots or canvas shoes with rope soles,—such as are
used at home for bathing shoes,—the latter seeming to be great
favorites. These suits are quite picturesque and said to be
especially comfortable for horseback. One day we drove about
five miles in the country to visit the estancia of one Señor Mongrell, a native. The road was broad and poor, the sides of it
bright with red verbena blossoms, that plant being a native of
the country; now and then we drove through a little brook,
and passed the corner of the estancia of the Spanish consul,
which is sixty-three square miles in extent, and given up
entirely to grazing. The rich green fields are everywhere
separated by smooth wire fences, barbed wire being tabooed in
all these countries as a barbarous, cruel invention; and in the
fields were grazing a great many horses and cattle, as well as
some of the small native ostriches. Mongrell's estancia is given
over to raising young from imported cattle, to sell to other estancieros and improving his own stock. He had some fine
English and French stallions and mares, each in a big box-
stall. Some fine Durham and Holstein bulls and cows, and
quite a flock of merino sheep. The latter came from Vermont.
The house was a low adobe one, and faced on three sides of a
court. The center was the residence, and the wings for offices
and kitchens. There was a broad piazza to the residence, and
we sat there some time, talking to the pretty señora and her
children, the señor having unfortunately gone to a neighbor's,

so we missed him. Several neighbors rode up as we sat there, and maté was passed. As we drove back the country looked lovely in the afternoon sunlight, and we later enjoyed a dinner in Mr. Hufnagel's roomy patio, under the budding grape-vines, surrounded by flowers, and the moon so bright that the lamp was superfluous.

XX.

PAYSANDU AND THE CAPITAL OF ENTRE RIOS.

REMINISCENCES OF THE TYRANT URQUIZA—HIS ALTAR IN
THE CATHEDRAL—THE SPLENDID UNIVERSITY AT CONCEP-
CION—AN AMERICAN GIRL'S KINDERGARTEN.

OUR next visit to Paysandu was made a year later, and we
found the town looking much the same as it did the year
before, only this time we came in the season when balls and
operas were the order of the day. We went to a ball given by
a Club, and it was a most creditable affair. The rooms were
good-sized, well-decorated, the music good, the supper the
same, and the very best families there to dance with. The
only dances they have which are different from ours are a
quadrille and the danza. In the quadrille every one stands
up in two long lines, the music begins to play, and you begin
to bow—every few steps you bow, and in fact you cannot bow
too often ; it is the essence of the dance. The danza is a

round—well, not a round dance, but a round walk-around.
The music is slow and pretty, with the sound of castanets
in it. One takes two short steps to one side, turns half
around, and then takes two steps in another direction, keeping it up any length of time, and dancing it without any
trouble. The opera-house is large, fairly well appointed,
and would be comfortable if these people would only once
acknowledge that they have a winter and prepare for it. Then
they would close up some of the cracks in the partitions, shut
the doors, and warm the place. As it is, we sat in our heaviest
wraps, with shawls over our knees, and heard " Faust " and
" Ernani " very well sung. The set for the garden scene for
" Faust " was a patio with a tiled cistern in the center, and
all the plants set out in tubs and kerosene cans, which undoubtedly struck the native as quite the proper thing, and it
did not look badly.

The only town on the right bank of the Uruguay is ten
miles below Paysandu and is called Concepcion del Uruguay,
for two reasons : firstly, because it is popularly supposed to be
on the river, and, secondly, to distinguish it from another Concepcion in the Argentine Republic. The city used to have a
good port, and as it was the capital of the province of Entre
Rios, had a good deal of trade, but an island formed in front
of it and has grown until now only the smallest trading vessels can make their way up the narrow, shallow channel to

the wharves, and everything of any size must anchor in the river some three miles away.

A railway has been built from Parana, on the Parana River, the new capital of the province, to this city, and the railway company, has run a long mole and wharf away out to the recent deep anchorage. We landed at this, and the railway authorities kindly sent down a hand-car, which took us to the shore end of the mole, where a carriage was waiting. Just here there are two large brick buildings, one of them a custom-house and the other for the use of the captain of the port, and we went in to call on the last-named official. He was a pleasant man of the usual Spanish type in appearance, and the most conspicuous article on his writing-table was a big Colt's revolver, placed there, perhaps, as a compliment to the *Norte Americanos.*

The roads are splendid and we drove quickly over one of them across the intervening plain, and were whirled into the town and up to the main plaza, where we alighted and began to explore. Entre Rios, like most of the other provinces when the Argentine was a confederation, and not a republic, as it is now, had its share of tyrants, but he who eclipsed them all was Gen. Jose Urquiza, shining second only in the infamous constellation to Juan Manuel Rosas, of Buenos Ayres, and being rivaled by Lopez, of Paraguay. Urquiza managed to get possession of most of the land in the province and lived like a czar.

His grand palace was at San Jose, about ten miles from Concepcion, but on one side of the plaza we saw a large, fine house, known as his town palace, and it is by far the finest residence in the city. We caught a glimpse of a lovely patio through the open gate, but some of the family were living there, which prevented our going farther in. One side of the plaza was occupied by the cathedral and university, standing side by side. The latter is a famous institution, and had been established thirty-six years the 28th of this July. Youths from all this part of South America attend it, and it is so well endowed by the general government that even the poorest ambitious young man has a chance, for the charges are only ten nationals a year, and a small matriculation fee. The buildings are large and comfortable, the corps of professors numerous, and said to be excellent, while the regular and elective courses of study seem very comprehensive. They have a drill-room, gymnasium, and good showing of apparatus in the chemistry department. The museum has a fine collection of fossils, agates, and petrifactions gathered in the province, and is presided over by a most enthusiastic Frenchman, one of the professors.

There are a great many schools in the city, and a normal college. At the latter is one of our countrywomen in charge of the kintergarten department. The cathedral is large, and the interior would be beautiful if the cheap, tawdry altars were eliminated. Only one has any claims to beauty : that belongs

11

to the Urquiza family, and is to the left of the high altar. It is quite pretty with its many silver ornaments, and near it, in the wall, the tyrant is buried. A marble tablet over him bears an inscription which informs one that here lie the remains of Gen. Jose Urquiza, who was assassinated at his palace of San Jose at 7:30 in the evening, the 11th day of April, 1870, aged sixty-nine years, and that this tablet is erected to his memory by his sorrowing widow and children. If his fate had only found him out about fifteen years earlier there would have been fewer widows and orphans in Entre Rios by several hundred, for his path was strewn with the corpses of those he hated, disliked, or could not bend to his will.

The city is large and spreads a long distance out over the plain, but there is nothing of especial interest in it, and the only industry, besides teaching, is an aguardiente factory. The plaza is unusually large and was gay with flower-beds, besides having many good-sized trees, whose shade was refreshing, and underneath one was a tiny little beer garden, with just room for two tables. Besides the cathedral, university, and Urquiza palace, the penitentiary, Jefe Politico's building, theater, and the largest hotel in the place, all front on this plaza. We were driven out to see the railroad station, which is white and dazzling to the eyes, as it is quite new, and not a bit of green near it, and the sunshine pouring down upon it.

XXI.

UP THE RIVER URUGUAY.

NUEVA PALMYRA.

WEALTH OF LITTLE WORTH TO AN EXILE—A TYPICAL "FORTY-NINER"—A SUBURBAN HORSE RACE—THE GIRL WHO PLAYED A WHOLE OPERA ON THE PIANO.

ON one of our trips up the River Uruguay, our anchor dropped just in front of the sleepy-looking little town of Nueva Palmyra. Three wharves jut out into the river from the stretch of sandy beach, and while they are all good to land at, the shore end of each dumps one in the sand, for the beach runs two or three streets back into the town, and these streets are less well provided with sidewalks than any others in the village. But once the hard ground is reached the walking is very pleasant, and the first day we wandered all about the streets. The ground slopes toward the river, and in a few places it is quite steep, so by pausing when we reached a summit, every here and there, pretty views of broad river, flat islands, and rolling country met and pleased the eye. The houses are the usual one-story brick affairs, covered with adobe, and relieved from perfect ugliness by the occasional trees in the front and blooming plants in the patios. Many of the trees were orange, and loaded with fruit and blossoms. The deathly stillness of the place was most disagreeable ; the ground was so soft that horses and people passed like specters ; only the barking of the dogs broke the pall-like silence. The main plaza is heavily shaded by pine as well as eucalyptus trees, the sod beneath them plentifully bestrewn with the red and yellow blossoms of wild oxalis, and there were several seats near the paths. Resting awhile on one of them, we were first interviewed by the dogs, and there were any number of them, for the commonest sight in this part of the world is a bunch of dogs. Every inhabitant must own several. Some are well-bred, but the predominating canine is a small, intelligent, yellow cur.

After the dogs had finished their inspection came the children, wonderfully pretty ones, too, and among them, a boy with an ideal Italian face and a lithe little figure. He was about six years old and hugged tight to his little breast a pair of big chickens, which he shyly confided to us he wanted to sell for thirty-five cents the pair, and when we took them he was too busy looking at us to count the money in his chubby little fist.

I suppose he wondered what we wanted them for, and certainly they were an embarrassing acquisition until fortune favored us by sending a man along who was willing to take them to the gringo's boat.

Facing the plaza were the usual police barracks, a drug-store, post-office, dwelling-houses, and church. The latter was the most forlorn building of the kind that I ever saw ; small, its bricks uncovered and chipped off, the tower just carried a few feet above the roof and abandoned. Doves circled above it and had their nest built in the places where the beams of the builder's scaffolding had left holes. The door stood wide open, and, entering, we finally made out in the obscurity a brick floor full of traps for unwary feet, a few wooden benches, three poor altars and a preaching pulpit draped in crocheted lace. Glass was lacking and the window spaces were covered with cloth, the consequence being that the darkness could almost be felt. Later we saw in the street a solitary priest, and for forlornness and shabbiness of aspect he matched the church.

As is usual in Uruguay, there was excellent shooting all about the town, quail, doves, duck, and snipe abounding, and as a gentleman of English descent, and a true sport, placed himself, his dogs, and lands at our disposal, we lived on game until we cried out " *pas toujours de perdrix.*" His house was not far from town, so one Sunday afternoon we walked out there. Our way led us through the quiet little town, which looked as usual ; but when we emerged on to the plain beyond it, we saw some thirty men mounted on the wiry, small horses of the country watching with much interest a scrub race, which finished just as we joined a knot of men on foot, among whom were some of our friends.

The winner was a pretty sorrel horse, and his owner, a lieutenant of police, was jubilant because he had made twenty dollars. This was evidently considered big stakes, and a pilot, who had come up with us, was much amused at having won twenty cents from a man who was very noisy and anxious to bet against the sorrel, but evidently cautious when it came to a practical backing of his opinion. Leaving them, we walked over the green slopes, which were cropped close by a large flock of sheep that were wandering about.

Finally we turned into one of these bits of road, and at the farther end found a big swinging gate set in the wire fence. From this the road led us through the barnyard and orchard to the long house with thatched roof, where we were cordially welcomed by our host, who always wears high boots, corduroys, a velvet coat and chimney-pot hat, the quiet, pleasant Señora Pepa, his wife, whom he has never allowed to learn English, and their fourteen dogs. The house had a long, low porch along the front, the floor of which was even with the outside ground, and, like those of the rooms, formed of badly-laid tiles. Everything was plain, and oh, so lacking in comfort! I gazed

in astonishment, for he has land in large tracts, the rent from
some of them bringing him in $3,200 a year, and that alone
would have given them comforts, but it was an illustration of
how indifferent we become when isolated from our kind, and
how easy it is to lapse into barbarism of life, if not of mind.
His mind was bright and trained, he was well up in the doings
and sayings of the world of to-day, but his house was behind his
mind by several centuries.

There was one United States citizen in the place, who claimed
to have been a good deal of a rolling-stone, and the hirsute
appearance of his head gave one the impression that he—contrary to tradition—had gathered a good deal of moss. He said
he was a "forty-niner," and left California to go to Chili and
help Enrique Meiggs build railroads; after that it was a short
journey for him across the Andes to the Argentine, and here, as
there were no obstacles on the level pampas to call a halt, the
wind blew him clear across country to the river, and crossing
that he landed in Uruguay, where he had prospered and soon
intended returning to California to settle down. He had peculiar ideas on the subject of medicine; thought gunpowder the
great cure-all. I supposed he meant taken *via* a pistol barrel,
but he did not; he meant swallowed or rubbed in.

As we go through life we gradually learn a great deal. I
learned, by eating a bit of whale, that life was too short to
spend in eating peculiar things simply to say you had done so;

and in Nueva Palmyra I learned not to ask a girl to play the piano. I here asked a healthy girl of fourteen if she would not *tocar* a little, and she was so kind as to hammer away one hour and a half. She played an opera straight through with never a stop, and we thus unavoidably made a rather long call, especially as our dinner was spoiling on board.

XXII.

FRAY BENTOS.

LIEBIG'S EXTRACT A GREAT URUGUAYAN INDUSTRY—HOMES
OF THE WORKMEN—THE PROCESS OF MANUFACTURE.

THE twin towns of Fray Bentos and Independencia, each built
on a point that juts sharply out into Uruguay River, are quite
pretty from a distance—the gray houses and green fields, the
curving beach between, and back of the latter a road, dotted
with houses its whole length. We went ashore at Independencia and found it like the usual river town—a good wharf, a
number of short, unpaved streets, with here and there a stretch
of flag or brick sidewalk, a few stores, the window of one or
more filled with silver ornaments for harness, whip-handles, and
maté bombillas, many one-storied houses, more or less clean and
more or less ornamented, according to the wealth of the owner.
We quickly walked through it one cool autumn morning,
stopping a few moments to enjoy the view of rolling country
covered with green clover from the pretty plaza which lay just

at the top of a steep slope, and taking the road along the river soon reached Fray Bentos.

Fray Bentos is quite a little town, and is entirely owned by the Liebig Company. All their extract of beef is made there, and the houses are occupied by their workmen. We passed several of these houses on our way to the main entrance of the works, and they looked cleanish and comfortable, with little flower-gardens in front and a cistern of adobe gleaming white among the flowers. Near the large gate was an office, and here we were received by Mr. Webster, the cashier, as it was too early for the superintendent, who arrives between 10 and 10:30. Mr. Webster showed us the offices and then the long, large board-room. In the center was a long table with big chairs around it, that are used by the board when it meets. On two of the walls hung maps of four out of the five large estancias owned by the company and devoted to raising cattle for their factory. But large as they are, they cannot supply the demand, and great numbers have to be bought all over the country, they paying on an average from $10 to $12 a head for good beasts. One side of the room was lined from floor to ceiling with bookshelves, and on them was a library for the benefit of the employés. At the farther end stood a large sideboard with specimens of the products of the factory, just as it was when placed in the last world's exhibition in Paris. There were two rows of different-sized jars filled with the extract that every one knows so well, a jar of tallow and another of dried beef in powder, and yet a third of bone dust, also tins of corned beef and of beef tongues. There was a large, fine room adjoining this, which is used by Mr. Crocker, an Englishman, the superintendent of the works. He has a nice house surrounded by pretty grounds, but he evidently deserves the place with all its emoluments, for everything seemed in excellent order, and as clean as possible wherever we went.

Leaving this building, we entered the main yard, and first passed the meat-shop, where several animals are cut up and dealt out each day gratis to the workmen. Just beyond was a long, low shed, with a sloping floor, paved with flagstones. Blood stood between all the stones, and there were some men busy trying to wash it out with hose and water. We were just too late to see the killing, they having stopped two or three days before, for which I was truly thankful. We entered the shed, and at one end, mounting a few wooden steps, stood where the killing takes place. It was small, just about room enough for four men to stand, and in front of us was a small circular stockade, and into this about a dozen cattle are driven at a time. The loop end of a rawhide lasso is dropped over the horns of one of the animals by a man on the platform. The other end is attached to the shaft of a small stationary engine, which revolves quickly and draws the struggling animal into the short passage and up to the feet of the butcher who, stooping over, with one blow of a short, heavy, dagger-shaped knife, severs the spinal cord just back of the head. The beast drops on to the floor of the passage, which is a flat car and runs on a track out into the open shed. Here the animal is rolled on to the stones, a man seizes it, disembowels, skins, and cuts it into quarters. These are the employés who make the most money. They are paid fifteen cents an animal, and make from $175 to $200 a month. The heads, hoofs, and horns are taken to the bone-dust factory, the quarters are hung on hooks on long racks near by and cut up, the best parts sent to the beef-extract house, the others to the corned-beef factory; the tongues to still another building, where each one is split and canned; the hair from the tails to still another building, where they are packed in bales, and the hides to vats at the farther end of the shed, where they are pickled and tanned.

The vats were full of hides in different stages, and after looking at them we went into the building where most of the beef is boiled in immense covered vats. When it is cooked all the broth is taken and carried to the extract-house, where it is mixed with the selected portions of the animal, like the tender-loin, which have been minced to a pulp in hash machines. No grease is present, as all the fat is cut off to make tallow. The pulp and broth are boiled in open tanks with steam radiators at the bottom. It is in each tank two hours and then passes to another. After boiling all day it is done, and is put up in 100-

VICTORY SQUARE. BUENOS ARES.

pound tins and sent by ship to Antwerp, where it is packed into
the small jars that we are familiar with. They kill about six
months in the year, beginning in December, and average 1,000
animals a day, employ 300 men all the year and 700 in the killing season. The workmen are mostly Italians and Basque
Spaniards. We visited the other buildings, the engine-room,
piles of coal, and wharves, at which lay several vessels loading;
but there was nothing unusual about them except their large
size and the smells. There are more and stronger smells to the
square inch in Fray Bentos than any place I ever visited.
Cologne is not a patch on it; they were varied and all awful.
Even the pores of our skins seemed filled, and I walked the dock
in a strong wind for several hours after bathing before I ceased
to abhor myself. I should hardly care to work there even if
wages are paid promptly. A house only costs from four dollars to five dollars a month, and even a stranger can buy a
whole tenderloin for ten cents. The company was started with
much difficulty—because no one would believe in it and buy
stock—in 1865, has ever since been prosperous, and pays good
dividends, besides all the lives the extract has saved.

There are a good many colonies near the river and some are
flourishing, notably the German one at Nueva-Berlin and a
French one some three leagues from Colonia, but the govern-
ments are not pleased because so few immigrants become citizens. All their children born in the country are claimed, but

I met quite a number who told me they were Orientals or Argentines, because they were born in the country, but when they went back to Europe they would also be citizens of their father country.

XXIII.

AFLOAT ON THE PARANA.

A RIVER OF WONDERFUL WIDTH AND NUMBERLESS ISLANDS.
—A GREAT COUNTRY FOR SHEEP—LUXURIOUS LAMB-
ROASTS—IMMENSE HERDS OF CATTLE AND HOW THEY
ARE LASSOED—IMPORTED AMERICAN STOCK.

Down the Uruguay we glided until we came to the mouth of the Parana River, known as the Guazu, and entering it were upon the surface of a mighty waterway, whose bosom is so broad that you must make your way some eleven hundred miles against the current, before both banks are visible at the same time. Opposite the city of Rosario it is forty-five miles wide, and that is about 150 miles from the mouth. The residents we found always spoke of going to the coast instead of to the river bank, which would not have seemed so odd if the vast expanse of water spread out unbroken before them, but it does not. The channel is so full of islands that the effect is that of a network of narrow water-courses instead of one grand sweeping mass. The water is of a tawny shade because of particles of sand and earth that are carried along by it and form the islands. A stick that lodges will start an island and a wreck off a port will form a bar so quickly that the port is soon closed unless it is prevented by removing the obstruction. At the same time the current is so swift that it cuts away old islands with the greatest rapidity once chance begins the work. Pilots are a necessity, and only those who are always upon the river will take a vessel of much draught above Rosario.

The islands naturally are all low, and they are densely covered with a growth of grass and low trees. They are the home of the nutria, whose skin is so prized by the makers of felt hats, and which are hunted by men in boats, armed with guns or spears, and assisted by dogs. The boats are rowed to a likely island and the dogs sent in along the shore. On finding an animal they engage it in combat, being seconded by their masters, who arrive as soon as possible, for the nutrias fight stubbornly, and the dogs often get badly bitten. Numerous snakes are in the underbush, and a small bird of greenish-yellowish plumage often alighted on the vessel. I was told that tigers—*i. e.*, leopards—were also to be found on the islands, and I do not doubt it, but none ever ventured forth to the edge as we were passing. There are numbers of capinchos, an animal that looked to me like a cross between a pig and a beaver. They live on land, and spend much time in the water. By some their flesh was said to be delicious to eat, that it tasted like pork, while other authorities as solemnly assured me it was horrid stuff, not even fit for the natives. The reader may take his choice. I never tried it. I used to enjoy watching the camelotes, or floating islands of weeds, sometimes of great extent, moving along with the current, making their way down toward the ocean, the vegetation growing and weeds blossoming quite undisturbed by the journey.

The river drains such an amount of territory that it is often high and often low, and vessels ashore are a very common sight. Let a sailing ship anchor to wait for a fair wind, and she may or may not be afloat when the wind comes ; and once aground, a bank will form around her so rapidly that her bones may lie there until they become exposed and bleach.

Just below the mouth stretch the flats of Martin Garcia, where wrecks and vessels ashore were always to be seen, and the last time I passed over there were twenty-five vessels beached, some of them large steamers, making quite a fleet in distress. The channel is buoyed, but the channel shifts, the buoys shift, and there you are.

Before we came to any town our anchor generally dropped just in front of the estancia " El Ombu," where we were sure of a warm welcome from, and some charming days with, Mr.

and Mrs. Kenyon, English people. The bank was bluff, and from the top edge the ground extends back in an unbroken plain to the horizon. Sheep are raised, and there were always large flocks of them feeding on the green grass and clover, each herd guarded by a man on horseback, while all about were numbers of horned plover, hawks, turkey-buzzards, and little gray owls that lived in burrows in the ground. There was an old house near the coast, which was kept in excellent repair, and had nice orange trees in front, but the mosquitoes were so bad that they were forced to build again, and moved about a mile and a half inland, quite near to the railroad station of El Paraiso, which is on the main line between Buenos Ayres and Rosario. Several large ombu, a row of eucalyptus, and an orchard of peach trees marked the house, which was, as usual, of one story, and covered a good deal of ground, besides the numerous out-buildings, which were all detached. Here we were treated to all the national dishes, were taken driving over the plain, went for duck and bird shooting, and had *asados,* when a lamb would be skinned, cleaned, and then roasted whole on a long iron rod—*asador*—one end of which was driven into the earth before an open fire. It was delicious food, and made gluttons of us all.

There were between 43,000 and 45,000 sheep that grazed over three square leagues of land, valued at $240,000 a

square league. Clover was plenty, but the land was divided
into sections by wire fences, and each field given a rest.
Their thirst is slaked by water pumped into troughs in
the different fields by the herdsmen, gauchos, peons, or whatever you choose to call them. The adjoining estancia was
owned by a Señor Martinez de Hoz, of Buenos Ayres, and
here, as at many other estancias in the country, we were
sure of a cordial greeting. Once I remarked that I had
never seen an animal lassoed, and as a consequence we
were invited, about a baker's dozen of us, to breakfast,
and quite early in the morning were taken to see a herd
rounded up and some cattle selected out of it by a pur-
chaser from Buenos Ayres. When we reached the spot we
found a large bunch of cattle surrounded by cow-boys, who
were riding swiftly in an outer circle. Senor Martinez de
Hoz and the buyer were near, and when an animal was
selected by the buyer he would point it out, one or two
cow-boys would dash in and bring the desired creature out
of the confused mass, and, once it was out, the point was
to keep it from returning, so a man would ride around it
in circles until it was a good distance away and joined
to those already selected. When this was finished Señor de
Hoz told two of the men to take their lassos and catch
me an animal. I had seen pictures of mad steers chased
by picturesquely dressed gauchos, careering like mad over

a plain; had read of the wonderful feats of catching an
animal here or there on any projecting angle, until it
seemed to me as if it must be a spectacle to make the
heart beat high and the breath come short, and now I was
to see this wonderful thing. Here was everything as I
had pictured it in my mind; but alas for my anticipations!
instead of a mad, galloping chase over the prairie, what I
actually saw was two men ride up to the herd and stop
at the edge of the dense mass. For a moment they were
motionless, then one leaned over in his stirrups and dropped
the loop of his lasso over the horns of a bullock and towed
him out. The beast fussed, kicked, and resisted, but out
he came. Then I was asked where else he should be caught,
and as he had his head well down and in the way, I
said a front foot. Well, they worked a long while and
finally got it there, but I think he walked into one of the
numerous loops on the ground, as several other cow-boys
had joined in the affair. I suppose it was very dangerous,
for the cattle are wild, and I was not allowed to go far
from the carriage, while the gentlemen kept close by their
horses, as we all must be ready to mount and fly if the
herd made a rush our way. But no picture of lassoing will
ever please me again; the rush and dash and excitement all
vanished before the tame reality. A cow was killed, because
it had a tumor on its jaw, and we saw it skinned, the men

using the knives that they wear in their belts, the same that they use for eating and for killing their enemies.

We had a delightful breakfast, and then went through the stables to see the stock, which has been imported to improve the herds. Among the horses was a big black stallion, son of the American horse Foxhall. There were merino sheep from Vermont, some English horses, and a bull. In front of the house was a large aviary, filled with native wild birds caught in the fields, and, just beyond, a charming garden, where we picked Parma violets, pansies, phlox, hyacinths, carnations, and mignonette, and where the gardeners wage eternal warfare against swarms of ants. There are about two square leagues in this estancia, and, as elsewhere, the herds are watched by gauchos, who live in little mud huts placed at convenient distances about the fields and called puestos. A great deal of maize is raised about here, chiefly for use on the estancias.

XXIV

UP THE GREAT RIVER TO THE MODERN CITY OF ROSARIO.

ELECTRIC LIGHTS AND PUBLIC SCHOOLS—THE IRISH AS WOOL-
GROWERS—NEW DOCKS AT ROSARIO—SOCIETY FOR THE PRE-
VENTION OF CRUELTY TO ANIMALS.

THE little town of San Pedro, on the right bank of the Parana, was the next point of interest as we went on our winding
way up stream. Standing on the top of the low bluff, its
white houses and church gleaming in the sunshine, it always
looked bright and neat, but bare, almost indecently so to one
accustomed to trees and foliage, that soften while beautifying
the angular lines of the architect and mason. Instead of being
dedicated to St. Paul, which would seem a natural sequence,
the next river hamlet boasts the good St. Nicholas as its sponsor
and patron, and has thriven until it is the third city in the
province of Buenos Ayres. There are a good many buildings
scattered here and there along the edge of the bluff between the

towns, and from most of them a chute runs down to the water, by which sign we know that they are store-houses for the reception of hides and wool, mostly the latter. Sometimes they are full to overflowing, for wool-raising is one of the chief occupations in the Argentine Republic, and ocean steamers can lie alongside these bluffs and load, taking the raw material thence direct to the looms of Europe. I was told that the Irish were the fathers of the sheep industry, and that many had made large fortunes in it. There certainly are numbers of that nation resident in the country, and some of the Irish Porteñas whom we met were charming girls, with a delightful Irish brogue, although born and brought up in the Argentine, all of which has nothing to do with our sheep; so *revenons a nos moutons*, which in this case is the town of San Nicolas.

An island has formed in front of the town, so the anchorage is some distance below, and it was quite a pull against a strong current up to the wharf, which we reached only to find that it was built to fit the river during a freshet, and there were no steps to make it fit low water, and so we passed it by and got ashore by climbing over the side and across the deck of a small trading sloop. There were a few buildings at the base of the bluff, and here we found the captain of the port, a charming gentleman, who took us into his inner sanctum and gave us a great many compliments and much information. Maté was served to us, and as it is always boiling hot I tried to swallow quickly, for one needs a tongue in condition to wag when ashore abroad, but it was no use; it seemed as if a blister rose all the way down the tongue and throat in the wake of the fiery liquid, and the only vent to be found for my feelings was to disregard all signals to depart until each member of the party had swallowed their dose. There are about 15,000 inhabitants, all either well to do or rich, as they import very little and export a great quantity of wool, maize, and hides. There is a railroad station just behind the city where they can take the cars to Buenos Ayres to the southward, or Rosario to the north, and besides tapping the main line there is a short branch which goes to an inland town and brings much produce to the river.

A steep paved way guided us up to the main city, and here we found the streets of good width, laid out at right angles, well paved and lighted by electric lights; street-cars were running on the principal thoroughfares, the people looked healthy and happy, numbers of children were coming out of the public school buildings, and altogether everything except the low adobe houses looked American and nineteenth-century. The plaza was well shaded by trees and pretty, if one could forget the stucco monumental shaft in the center, which was painted blue and white, with an electric light on top. The church was closed, but the neat little inn alongside was not, and the beer—made in the country—deliciously cold. The market was empty except some meat, and we stopped at a corner to see the stage start for Mananzalita, thirteen leagues inland; the vehicle was a small antiquated affair painted yellow and drawn by six white horses, harnessed four abreast and two leaders. They were untamed creatures and gave any amount of trouble before they finally consented to all start at the same time, the driver meanwhile flourishing his whip and giving us a chance to acquire some very choice expressions in hybrid Spanish.

Rosario is the second city in the republic, and is not only a city of the present, but also of the future. It is well situated at a point which can be reached by large ocean vessels, while above the city the river is so uncertain as to its depth, even in the main channel, that large vessels dare not venture; hence about all produce brought down for abroad is landed and reshipped. It is also quite a railroad center, will become still more so in time, and is a great point for shipping goods into the interior by wagon. Large docks are being built, slowly, to be sure, but surely, and the wood—*ñandubay*—used is so hard that it takes a long while to shape it. It is red and rings almost like metal when struck. It is brought down from the forests of the Grand Chaco.

From the river the city is lovely with its wharves, large yellow custom-house, and lines of streets that gradually ascend the bluff, while above an irregular sky-line of houses and trees, broken by the two towers of the cathedral, is all fascinating, and from its extent we hoped for much pleasure, only to be proportionately disappointed, as it proved to be dull and uninteresting in the extreme. The shops are long lines of storehouses, mere depots, filled with large boxes and some samples, the streets almost deserted, stretching long distances of uniform houses. The pavements were bad, and the poor horses that dragged the heavy loads up the bluffs and along the rough streets cannot live very long, they are so beaten and maltreated. Across a broad street, from the head of the wharf, stands the big two-storied custom-house, and beside it is a peculiarly steep street leading to the upper city.

It was always very painful for me to walk up or down that street, for it was filled from early dawn until late at night with a struggling, slipping crowd of over-burdened horses and oxen. The desperate struggle to plant their ill shod feet firmly, the jump under the sting of the lash, whose whistle filled the air at all times, the bend of the slender legs strained almost to breaking, all make a horrible sight; and steep as the street was we always made a rush to get up it and away. The Society for the Prevention of Cruelty to Animals was introduced into the country by the late ex-President Domingo F. Sarmiento, and it is taking root even in Rosario, but progresses slowly and seems to have begun with chickens—to prevent their being carried about by the legs—instead of horses.

Horses are fastened to the cart in a peculiar manner—first, the horse has a leather saddle put on him, which is very simple in make. They take a framework made of a straight piece of wood with two short pieces nailed at right angles on each end; to the underside are fastened two long, round cushions, filled with hair; these rest on the horse's back, one each side of the back-bone, and over the framework is nailed a piece of leather, while under and over are laid as many saddle-cloths as the owner chooses, the whole held in place by a very broad girth. A rawhide thong passes through a hole in the end of the pole of the cart, and this throng is tied to a ring in one side of the saddle. A primitive bridle and reins are added, and the cart is ready to start unless more than one horse is needed. If so, one end of a long rope is fastened to the saddle of another horse, and the other end to some part of the cart, generally the front edge. Sometimes there will be two or even three of these loose horses attached. The horse connected with the pole does the steering, and he is free to go in any direction, acting as he does on a pivot—the end of the pole. The driver rides this horse.

The plaza is a large, bare square, with a few trees and benches around the sides, two broken fountains, and in the center a monument, which consists of a tall, fluted column, with a statue of Liberty on top, holding the Argentine flag, while at each of the four corners of the pedestal is a life-sized statue of an Argentine patriot, with an inscription beneath. These inscriptions cannot be very encouraging to patriotic youths, as they state that Gen. San Martin died far from his country.

Gen. Belgrano died in misery, Rivadavia died expatriated, and Moreno died in mid-ocean—on a ship, I suppose. The cathedral was being built around a smaller one, so, while the outside was finished, we never penetrated into the interior, because of the piles of bricks, mortar, and dust that met us at the door.

Of all the crowds of Italian emigrants flocking to the Argentine shores, the province of Santa Fe, of which Rosario de Santa Fe, usually called Rosario, is the capital, seems to have attracted the Piedmontese, and these hardy, industrious people are going in for agriculture and fruit gardens, sending their children to the public schools, improving the province in every way, and benefiting the city by giving it a flourishing back country. The government is kind to settlers, and these Italians, who are used to the hard, bitter lot of the European peasant, get on very well. They are strong, quick-tempered, as ready with the knife and firearm as the natives are, and do not growl when arrested and detained in jail months or years on suspicion, for the right of habeas corpus is a dead letter, and tales of flogging and ill-treatment in the jails that I knew of, I would rather not dwell upon. But what can one expect when police and the file of the army are recruited from convicts. A policeman in the Argentine never seemed to me to embody peace, law, and order, having broken all three. The Argentines have a splendid country, and they are making rapid strides, but like every one else, they are far from perfection.

XXV.

A TRIP TO CORDOBA.

A LAND VOYAGE OF DISCOVERY—THE WAKING CITY OF THE
PAMPAS—RELICS OF THE CONQUISTADORES—THE CATHE-
DRAL AND THE JESUITS' CHURCH—THE NUNS OF ST.
DOMINIC—STREET LIFE—MODERN IMPROVEMENTS.

ON the western edge of the vast Argentine pampas, deep set
in the dry brown bowl where once glistened and rippled the
waters of a lake, lies the quaint old city of Cordoba. Many
years it has lain there, "the world forgetting, by the world
forgot," its days of ancient glory having come and reached their
zenith before the Pilgrim Fathers landed on our shores. Some of
the old *conquistadores*, headed by Geronimo de Cabrera, march-
ing with the sword in one hand and the cross in the other, as
was their custom, came over the mountains from Peru and
down through Bolivia, reaching in 1573 this bowl-like site.
Seeing the pretty river rushing through it and the low range of
foot-hills standing protectingly near, they pitched their tents,

and soon the solid city rose, churches keeping pace with the
houses, the Jesuits even building a university and setting up a
printing-press, from which came ponderous old tomes in Latin,
Spanish, Quichua, and Guarani, the last two native Indian
languages, the books being used by the missionaries to spread
the gospel and teach the natives Spanish, and also containing
histories of the tribes and country. Would they were there
now! but the remorseless enemies of the Jesuits, who caused
them to be expelled from all the Spanish colonies, showed what
ignorance and vandalism their cloaks and cowls covered when
they burnt and destroyed the unique and invaluable library
that had cost their predecessors so much blood and labor to
accumulate and arrange.

Now the iron ribbon connects Cordoba with Rosario, and
thus with the outer world, and she is rubbing her eyes and
beginning to wake from her long nap; but there is still a
delicious old sixteenth-century flavor about her. Her streets
are narrow, and only the brilliant sunlight keeps them from
being gloomy; churches, convents, and religious property,
marked with some holy sign above the doors, abound. The
Cathedral is magnificent; standing at one corner of the lovely
old tree-shaded plaza, it is approached by broad steps and an outer
court; the two tall towers, with their clusters of bells, are of
adobe, worked and moulded into graceful shape with many
ornaments; part of the roof of the main aisle shows between

GROUP OF AMERICANS, CÓRDOBA, ARGENTINE.

them, while, behind all, the grand dome, looking like an imperial crown, rises to complete a lovely picture. The walls are smooth, but one can see in the outer ones where heavy uncut stones are set in, in courses, to give greater strength. The outer court is paved, and so is the portico, with old stones that show the tread of many feet ; but, once the quaint old wooden doors are passed, you meet the present age in a fine new-tiled floor ; it is beautiful and serviceable, but looks too new—as out of keeping as the new coarse frescoes that by their brilliant colors call your eyes away from the graceful curve of the arched roof of the aisles.

A short walk through the narrow 'streets, and we entered the court before the oldest church of all, that of the Jesuits. Its walls are dark and stained by wind and weather, but the adobe fairly shines in spots, it has worn so smooth. Two sad, drooping trees—*Quebracho blancho*—grow in the court, and a soft twilight pervades the interior, as if the church were in mourning for those who founded and built only to be ruthlessly driven out. The ceiling is superb; it is made of cedar that was brought from the distant mountains, on the backs of Indian converts, some two hundred and seventy years ago, then fashioned by their dexterous fingers and fitted in place without nail or screw. The church is in the shape of a Latin cross, the ceiling a Gothic arch, lined first with smooth, flat boards of the cedar, the surface then divided into spaces, richly ornamented by arabesques in gold and color; every few feet a broad, heavy moulding comes down from the apex, and following the curve ends at the base of the arch, where the wall begins; these divide the lines of arabesques and are ornamented sparingly with gold and color. The dome is large and panelled with cedar, the four lower corners being ornamented with good old paintings of the four Evangelists. Below the roof, running clear around the church, is a frieze of alternate portraits and coats-of-arms, but these had been painted on canvas and were in a terrible state of disrepair; those that one could make out seemed stern old Spaniards, clad in steel armor, but no one could tell me who they were. The old confessionals are fitted into niches in the ponderous walls, and the Jesuits, who have crept back one by one, although exiled by an unrepealed law issued the last time by Juan Manuel Rosas, President and Dictator of Buenos Ayres, are brushing up their old quarters, gilding heavily the crown-like sounding-board that hangs above the preacher's desk, and trying to spoil the general effect by filling the floor space with wooden benches. The gold used on the ceiling was brought from Peru, and that same favored country furnished the paints that were used with such charming effect. A small side-door leads into a narrow street, and if one looks back after leaving it, one sees over the portal in quaint old letters—

Casa de Dios,
Puerto del Cielo.

Which is in English—

The House of God,
The Gate of Heaven.

There is another door, which now is always barred and bolted, but once it led into their sunny old cloisters and garden, where the sun still shines, the fountain plashes and gurgles, the orange trees grow and are loaded with their golden fruit, while below them bloom and fade many lovely roses; thence a stairway leads to the old library, where some of their books stand on the shelves, having been rescued and returned. Beneath it is the old hall, at one end of which still hangs a Holy Family; and facing this, a full-length oil portrait of Bishop Trejo in canonicals. He was a native of Paraguay, and in 1613 founded the university, giving all his fortune of $40,000 for the purpose. The cloisters, gardens, and vaulted recitation-rooms still echo to the voices of youths being fitted for the battle of life; but instead of low-voiced monks in flowing robes, they are guided and taught by German professors, imported by the general Government, and paid by the same power, so that instruction is received at merely a nominal cost. A very pleasant set of learned gentlemen are the professors, and

13

they have had built a large, fine building, which adjoins
the old one and has a beautiful front on Calle Ancha,
the one broad street in the old city.   One of · the large
new rooms has a fine collection of birds, among which are
the only pair of bright-green eagles that I ever saw, and
wonderful humming-birds, one of them having a semicircle
of feathers, somewhat like those in a peacock's tail, standing out from each side of his little body.   There were all
the game birds of the country, some of them resembling
ours as California fruit resembles that of the Eastern States
—larger, of the same outward appearance, and much less
flavor.   The professor of botany has also a most wonderful collection of the flora of the country, which he has
wandered many hundred weary miles to collect.

Near at hand is the church of Santa Catalina, with a famous
nunnery attached, and, making an excuse of the fact that we
wanted to get some bamboo and horsehair *bombillas,* that the
nuns make, we looked for some time for an entrance to the
convent, and not finding it we went into the church, which is
very large, like all the churches in the city, lofty, and decorated
in good taste.   It is profusely illustrated, if I may use the expression, with scenes from the life of the patron saint, and she
seems to have had a most uncomfortable time.   There was a
gallery over the door with gratings and cloth screen; this is
what the nuns occupy when they sing the services, but there

was no entrance to it from the church, and we could not find
any one in the body of the church, behind the high altar, nor
in the small room to the right. There was a revolving cupboard
in the wall there, but repeated knockings brought no one. At
last in an alcove, in a small room on the left of the high altar,
his cloak wrapped around him, sound asleep, we found a priest;
we waked him, and told him in our choicest Castilian what
we wanted, and he not only told us the way to the inner court,
behind some houses, but followed, and helped us to interview
the sister who answered my knock on the turn-table. I never
saw an article of wood so tightly fitted and yet which turned
with such ease as this cupboard-like affair. I could hear a pleasant voice and musical laugh, but not a glimpse could I catch of
the nun, who promised that if we would return in the afternoon
she would see what she could do. When we returned, I told
her I was the foreigner who wanted the *bombillas*, and she put
a bunch of keys in the cupboard for me to give the portress,
while she went to speak to the Lady Superior. A quiet-looking
woman, shrouded in a manta, whom I had noticed sitting in
the court, came forward, and taking the keys, led us to a small
door in the corner next the church, and, unlocking it, let us
into a long, narrow room, perfectly dark, except for the light
that came through the door. At one end hung an old picture
of the Madonna and Child, dressed in stiff gold brocade, and
opposite a portrait of St. Dominic, clad in the same stiff drape-

ries that were such favorites with some of the earliest of the old masters; otherwise they were lovely. Along the wall between them was a row of chairs, and when we sat down we faced an iron grating that occupied the entire length of the room, and was fastened into the floor and the ceiling. It was made of flat bands, riveted quite close together, and about five feet inside of this was a similar one, inside of that a thick cloth veil. Soon we heard the turning of a lock somewhere, and then two female voices spoke. I had quite a long conversation with them, and found they knew all about themselves and their order, but nothing else. They are a branch of the order of St. Dominic, and this house was founded by one of the *conquistadores* in 1613; there are only rooms for forty nuns, and as soon as one dies another stands ready to enter, yet they draw only from the best families, and are strictly cloistered, living, dying, and being buried within the walls. They said they were happy, but their voices had a hollow sound, as if they came from the tomb, and I involuntarily pressed close against the outer railing as if to get nearer the unfortunates, for whom my heart was filled with pity when I thought of all they had renounced, and what their lives must be.

La Marced is another large church, and has a monastery attached. The monks wear a white habit, and looked very picturesque as we saw them, through a half-open door, pacing to and fro beneath the trees in the sunny garden. The church was being repaired, and only one altar was in order; before that about a dozen young brothers were chanting a service, keeping their eyes on us instead of their books; but they knew it all so well that they made no mistake. There was a horrible looking statue of a saint over one altar; he had been split open and cleaned out, but to judge by facial expression, was still alive. San Francisco Church was entirely closed for repairs, and the only other big church we entered was Saint Dominic's, which has a *repoussé* silver front to the high altar and a fine old pulpit; it also has a Gothic wooden altar, prettily carved, underneath which is a passage into the monastery. The orphanage opposite the Jesuit church is in charge of some sisters, who have a large number of little unfortunates under their care.

We visited two of the markets, but found very little of native manufacture in them; some rough pottery, coarse blankets, gayly-colored saddlebags of wool, and some coffee-colored lace, was about all. The lace was soft and pretty, with an immense amount of labor on it, and not very fine after all. In the streets only the richest women wear bonnets or hats, the rest use the black cashmere manta that is so common in Peru and Chili. It is a piece of cloth about nine feet long, and four to six in width, wound around the head and shoulders, enveloping the person as far down as the waist; a perfectly plain skirt is generally worn with it. Many of the men wear the old *gaucho* dress except the boots, which were formerly made by peeling the hides off an animal's legs, pulling them while still warm and soft over their own feet and legs, and leaving them to dry on and shrink into shape. Now they wear rough leather boots or low shoes, the latter made of canvas and rope, like those sold for bathing with us. The legs are covered with white cotton-cloth drawers that come down to the ankles, and are often embroidered, fringed, or otherwise ornamented nearly up to the knee; the poor simply wind a piece of cloth round their legs. These drawers are called *calconcillas.* As they would not be warm enough by themselves, a square of woolen cloth, varying from the coarsest woven sheep's wool up to very fine vicuña, according to the purse of the wearer, is taken; one straight side is fastened around the waist by a wide leather belt ornamented with big silver buttons; the short ends that are left hang down in front; the center of the straight side opposite that which is wrapped around the waist is brought up between the legs in front and tucked firmly under the belt; the two corners are left hanging loose. This garment is called the *chiripa*, and always looks as if it were going to drop off, but it does not; the square is large in order to give plenty of room when riding, and as a consequence, the bunch which does duty for the seat falls nearly to the wearer's ankles behind. A woolen shirt covering the upper part of the body, and hanging over one shoulder for convenience in carrying, or else regularly put on, is the *poncho* that all classes use more or less. This is often very fine and finished with a deep knotted fringe; it is simply a square of cloth, with a slit in the centre through which the wearer puts his head. A handkerchief knotted around the throat, some kind of a soft wool hat, and a sharp-pointed knife thrust into the belt complete the costume. When mounted on their small, wiry horses, the lasso, a coil of rawhide rope, at the saddle, riding rapidly and flourishing the thong-like whip that hangs from the wrist, their dress looks picturesque and suitable; but once they dismount and begin to walk, one sees it is but a swaddling for the form, clumsy, ungainly, and, like most native dresses, with no attention paid to shape, and the object of covering for warmth but imperfectly attained.

There is a nice theater, of good size, near the plaza, where an excellent company was giving Italian opera. There are two large plazas; the original one being filled with fine old trees, underneath which one can sit on comfortable benches and listen to a magnificent military band of some sixty well-trained musicians; the other plaza is quite distant, but it is lovely, for it is nearly all lake, only room for a shaded walk around the outside, and in the center one sees a small island with a grotto on it; and on this island on feast-days and holidays they burn set pieces of fireworks, their reflections in the water adding much to the effect. There is a promising Museum of the Province, that has just been started and put in charge of Padre Lavagna, a priest with a noble face, who had charge of a parish in the mountain region. His parish flourished; but while there he spent a good deal of time on botany, geology, and kindred subjects, reading Darwin's works and other like books, seeking more light on his favorite pursuits. A visiting priest saw them; he was reported and removed from his parish, which left him to starve until the Government held out a helping hand, giving him at the same time congenial work.

On the top of the bluff which makes the edge of the bowl that the city lies in, are two interesting buildings, the Observatory and Meteorological Bureau, both government institutions and both in charge of scientists from the United States. The Observatory was built during the Presidency of Gen. Domingo Sarmiento and has done some wonderfully good work, being not only well managed but the situation being exceptionally good for statistical work, in the Meteorological Bureau, which for so young an institution is progressing wonderfully. Its record shows an average of 65 per cent. of perfectly clear, sunny weather during the year in Cordoba. There is one disagreeable side to so much sunshine, and that is the clouds of dust, which fill the air at every puff of wind; it lies inches thick on everything that does not move, and when in the street even one's face is soon coated with it.

The hotels are not clean and not warmed, but the food is pretty good. Walking about the streets, one notices many bamboo-huts, the sides plastered over with mud and having thatched roofs, while towards the outskirts there are clusters and long lines of them; but now they are all doomed, and will be destroyed at the end of three months; a piece of land quite outside of the city having been set apart where the poor Indians can erect others. This is only one of the many schemes on foot to beautify the place. A plaza near the river was improved; a colossal equestrian statue, in bronze, of Gen. La Paz erected, and unveiled in the presence of the President, his Cabinet, and the foreign diplomatic corps, who all came from Buenos Ayres to assist. Just beyond the statue is a fine iron bridge, called the Marcos Juarez Celman bridge, in honor of the President; this bridge rests at either end on the splendid new embankment which will hedge the river in on either side when finished, and prevent the disastrous, fever-producing inundations that formerly came every spring when the snows of the Andes began to melt. On the farther side of the bridge a level space at the foot of the encircling bluff has been laid out as a park, and promises well. An immense dam and reservoir is building in the mountains for the purpose of irrigating the entire plain about the city so as to surround it with green fields and groves. There is a good race-course with a large grandstand, the boxes of which were filled with dark-eyed señoras and señoritas on the ninth of July, which is their Independence Day, when we saw some very fair races and an interesting crowd of countrymen, who had ridden in on their little horses and took a great interest in all the events of the day. The racers were mostly of English blood or imported stock crossed with native.

We happened upon a fair, and finding the girls in charge pretty, went in and invested. Nothing was for sale outright, but you handed one of the señoritas any sum you chose, and she gave you a greater or less number of tiny paper rolls, which were glued so tightly that it took some minutes to open each ; generally you found all blank inside, but one of the gentlemen found two numbers, after investing several dollars, and received a spool of pink cotton thread and a little picture with a prayer on the back. There were all sorts of bric-a-brac around the room with a number fastened to each, but those numbers did not appear to us nor to any of the other numerous gamblers in · the place. However, the girls were pretty and pleasant.

One of the residents, who was very kind to us, was an enthusiastic botanist, and showed us many curious things that were indigenous, among them the bark of a tree which could be scaled off in pieces no thicker than paper, making excellent cigarette wrappers. One day he proposed that we go to call on a friend of his in the country, and of course we were delighted. We rode through the city, and started to walk. It had not rained for months, the dust was ankle-deep and rose about us in a cloud. The road was very long, and I began to ask questions about the dust-laden shrubs and received a great deal of information in return. Some of them belonged to the cinchona family, others bore a seed vessel with a covering resembling tripe, and the bush is called monk's tripe.

Finally we arrived to find the usual low, white-washed country house, with numerous outbuildings, but this one was unusually blest in having numerous bright green fields about it, irrigated by the broad shallow river which flowed near by. The owner was absent, gone to the city, a peon informed us, and after expressing regret and disgust our guide proposed to take us home another way. I had been growing more and more amused as I watched the faces of our crowd, and felt ready for any lark, so agreed that we had better go home another way, and he led us across the green fields down to the river bank; he and I were about to step in and wade over when there was a revolution behind us and we had to go back the way we came.

Once in the hotel, I was treated to a piece of the mind of each of the party, my interest in shrubs belittled, and finally a demand was made to know if I had really intended wading that river, and I said, " Why not ? " I had already spoiled a blue cloth costume rather than hurt the feelings of our new friend, and saw no reason to hesitate at ruining a pair of shoes as well by wading, and as the water was not over half a foot deep, they would none of them have drowned. I was the only woman in the party, and the men did not like to show the white feather first, so I enjoyed their disgust and knew I could easily get even when necessary, as some spoke no Spanish and the others could not rattle it off as I could, and they often wanted help.

Cordoba is a most interesting place, and one could most pleasantly pass a month here, our nine days being altogether too short.   It is not yet modernized, and it is only by straying far from the regular routes in Europe that one can find such a charming, antique city to wander in as this, which is only to be reached by passing over miles and miles of dead level pampas; almost 250 of them, as the crow flies, lie between it, the city of Rosario, and the great Parana River.

In the streets of Cordoba only the richest women wear bonnets or hats; the others use the soft, black cashmere manta that is so common in Peru and Chili.   In Lima, the capital of Peru, it is the only recognized head-gear for church wear.   If you attempt to enter a sacred edifice with hat or bonnet on some one will ask you to take it off; bare heads or mantas are alone permissible.   This manta is a piece of cloth about nine feet long and four to six in width, wound around the head and shoulders, enveloping the person always as far as the waist and sometimes to the knees.   It is always of black, its fineness depending upon the purse of the wearer.   One sometimes sees women and young girls in a snuff-colored petticoat, leather girdle pendant, and white manta.   These are people who have taken a vow to wear the dress for a certain length of time, as a thank-offering for recovery from sickness of themselves or of some relative or friend. It is not assumed as a penance for terrible sins, as some assert, for I was repeatedly assured by native women in Peru that it was often put on as one would light a candle and put it before an altar, for any trivial religious reason. The women of South America are often spoken lightly of, and it seems to me quite without reason. If their men were like ours, if the women had our education and chances they would be as famous for their morality and beauty as is the girl of the United States. There, as everywhere, it is the one lamb who goes astray that is told of in song and story, not the ninety and nine in the sheepfold. After four years spent in South America, I am a warm defender of the women there. They are pretty, sweet, gentle, and pure, and their intellects good. What more can one ask?

XXVI.

FROM ROSARIO TO SANTA ELENA AND CITIES BY THE WAY.

PROFESSOR KEMMERICH'S BEEF-EXTRACT WORKS—AN ES-TABLISHMENT LARGER THAN LIEBIG'S—CAPTIVE INDIAN GIRLS AND WOMEN AS HOUSE SERVANTS.

JUST above the city of Rosario, the right bank of the Parana is a bluff and dotted with buildings, while the islands, being old, are well wooded, which makes them prettier than common, but this only lasts a while and we are soon winding and twisting among the shifting islands. The vessels we see are much smaller than those we saw below, and our craft had difficulty in obtaining a pilot, the one who had come from Asuncion three months before, declining to go, as the channel would be sure to have changed in that time. Diamante Point is a fine wooded headland, which we passed on the second day, and here it is that the naval academy was being placed, it having been decided to move the youths from their old quarters on one of the fine avenues of Buenos Ayres. While the location is healthy, and the view must be superb, yet it will seem a desert to the boys at first, and the tiny village nestling at the base of the river bluff of small account. We now found the left bank bluff all the way, and these bluffs are full of fossils, of all sorts and descriptions, from mastodons to tiny shells, the whole province of Entre Rios being a most famous place in which to search, all the museums of the country being well supplied from there. The city of Santa Fe, on the right bank, is large, but it is set so far back from the river that in passing one sees only the few buildings that form the port, whence a railroad runs to the city.

The city of Parana is just above on the Entre Rios bank, and here we tarried, anchoring close under a steep bluff, which is gradually being dug away to obtain the shells, just here mostly those of oysters, which lie in thick layers like veins, and are speedily converted into lime at the kilns near by. An oyster is not to be obtained in the markets of Uruguay or the Argentine, except a few that are brought down from Rio de Janeiro, yet here are millions of shells that must once have held the delicious morsels, and stopping by the bluff we dug out a few shells to take on board, because they reminded us of the pleasures to come when once more we should be *chez* Uncle Sam. Landing at the wharf, we passed several vessels loading with lime, and numerous ox-carts drawing the same to them. The street was a poor roadway, with a few houses here and there, and at the farther end we found a street-car, drawn by three horses—a spiked team —which was soon filled with people; then the driver cracked his long whip, shouted lustily to the poor brutes, and they dashed off, dragging the heavy car up the steep bluff, along a gently sloping street, about a mile and a half in all, into the city. The place is now, since the decadence of Concepcion del Uruguay, the capital of the province, the two cities being connected by rail. Paraña is thriving; it has a good port, which its rival has not, so all the produce from the interior comes there to be shipped; then, like most places in the country, there were all sorts of schemes on foot,—booms, one might call them,—while every one was cheerful and smiling, seeing a great fortune in the near future. To a stranger there was not much of interest, the same narrow streets that are found everywhere, high sidewalks, adobe houses with flat roofs, and shops for the sale of necessaries. A church with a crooked cross on top, unfinished without and bare within, faced the old plaza. The new plaza was farther up and looked rather pretty with its flower beds, while the singing of the children in the graded schools called our attention to the large building whence they soon came swarming to scatter in all the adjacent streets. One day we pulled down the river to where some railroad tracks came down to bring freight to ships, and wandered into the country, which we found covered with grass and low bushes. The views of rolling land and spreading river were quite pretty, and the cardinal birds whistled blithely as they flew from bush to bush. We were brushing off mosquitoes and wandering about rather aimlessly, when suddenly surrounded by a herd of goats, in charge of a tiny cherub-faced boy who was singing at the top of his voice something about the moon, until the song was frozen in his little throat by the sight of strangers; yet he soon forgot his fears and told us about his herd, finally running off after them with a smile and a cheery good-day to us.

Villa Urquiza is a little town named for the old tyrant, whose brother still lives there. It looked especially pretty as we glided past, because of the fringe of willow trees along the bank, underneath which were a number of people and carts, which gave it a lively air. There is quite a number of colonies on either bank, mostly formed by different nationalities and called the Swiss colony of Anna Maria Point, German colony of some other place, and they were all reported as flourishing, but generally sat well back from the river and were not easily accessible.

The next stop, to go ashore, was at Santa Elena, where is the large condensed beef-extract factory of Prof. Kemmerich, a

14

German, who was for many years head man under Mr. Giebert at Liebig's factory in Uruguay. He married one of Mr. Giebert's daughters, a charming woman, and we enjoyed several days here, mostly spent at the hospitable house of Prof. Kemmerich and his brother-in-law, Giebert, who is also in the business. There were two interesting Kemmerich girls, and each had an Indian waiting-maid of about her own age. I say about, as Mrs. Kemmerich told me she had no means of knowing the age of the children when given to her, for they were captives. The smallest one—about five years of age—was bought of her captor for a bottle of cane (native rum), and he gave no details to the friend who secured her. We often saw Indian girls filling the place of servants in families of officials, and, while they seemed always kindly treated—and those with her were certainly most kindly and considerately and even tenderly treated by Mrs. Kemmerich—still their position excited my curiosity. I was told by an Englishman who had been long years in the country, that the Indian tribes in the North were often troublesome, and when war was made on them the men were killed or enlisted in the army, while the women and children were brought to the river and started for Buenos Ayres ; that wherever the steamer stopped that had women captives on board the inhabitants could go to the authorities and get orders for what number they wished, then could go on board, pick out their women and take them away as their property—slaves, in short. He also told me that, finally, the foreigners found it out and were so distressed at the sights consequent on separating families that they protested until the government sent orders to take no more women and girls prisoners. I had the temerity to ask several Argentine officials about it, and am free to say their elaborate and explanatory denials were not altogether convincing, chiefly because they left the presence of the girls I had seen unaccounted for. The little one at the Kemmerichs' was bought from an Indian who was supposed to have captured her from some other tribe with whom his people were at war. Prof. Kemmerich is professor, doctor, and land-owner, as well as owner and head of a factory larger than Liebig's, where delicious extract is made, and he also puts up a peptonized extract and liquid concentrated bouillon, neither of which is prepared by Liebig. He is also German consul and a citizen of that empire. About the house is quite a colony of houses for the workmen as well as a schoolhouse where the children are taught. One day we went for a long ride in the country, and the roads near the settlement were a novelty to me. The thousands of animals driven to slaughter are about the same size, and when the road was softened by rains they had trodden it into furrows, each row stepping in the tracks of those preceding. Then the road had dried, which hardened it. Driving over this is to be imagined. Miss Kemmerich and I braced against one another and clung to the carriage with our hands, yet it was delightful, too, for the country was slightly rolling and fairly well wooded. There were numerous flocks of parrots and parroquets flying about, as well as doves and quail. We visited an estancia and watched and talked to the herders and their women and children, as well as saw a little of their home life. This was a farm house, and the contrast with any I ever saw in my own land was striking; the utter lack of cleanliness, comfort, or even what we would consider necessities, and the satisfaction of all hands with the existing state of affairs was appalling, yet these people were kind and hospitable, offering eggs and maté, which seemed their all.

XXVII.

LA PAZ TO CORRIENTES.

ITS QUAINT OLD STRUCTURES—THE CHURCHES, MARKETS,
AND PUBLIC BUILDINGS—CHAT WITH A BANK CASHIER
AND AN INTERVIEW WITH A NATIVE PRIEST—A TOWN
THREE HUNDRED YEARS OLD.

THE city of La Paz is quiet and peaceful, even if it is not
.the actual abode of the peace which passeth all understanding,
and shortly after we had anchored the pilot went on shore to
his home and sent me off, not a dove, but a live cardinal bird,
tied up in a handkerchief. The next day we went ashore to
find it quite a city, situated on ground sloping up from the
river, spreading out over a good deal of space, as there are
many trees and some orchards. There does not seem to be
much trade, and although the streets have been cut into deep
ruts by the wheels of heavy wagons, many were grass grown,
ruts and all. After our custom, we talked with the people in
the streets and shops, a wine merchant asking us back into his

house, where we found a pretty wife and a numerous brood of black-eyed little children, one of whom was several times offered to us, and they really seemed in earnest in so doing. The shops were small, but, as usual, there was a silversmith who hammered out pretty things for the adornment of man, woman, and horse. They are building a fine, large municipalidad or town hall, and the plaza had long lines of rose bushes, orange and eucalyptus trees. The country around was dotted with white houses, which looked pretty and cheerful.

From here we left the bluffs behind us, that is, we left the bank and struck out into the maze of islands, sometimes brushing close to them, and little birds were often brought me that had alighted on the deck or rigging. They were mostly like our yellow birds, and were so wild that we let them go when near the bank on either side.

The town of Esquinas was visible in the distance, over a low island which had formed in front and effectually blocked up the port to any but the tiniest craft. Bella Vista looked much like the other towns when we slowed down off it to send the mail ashore and get some marketing. The official visit of the captain of the port was made in a boat evidently hired for the occasion, as while he had two port sailors in uniform as attendants the man who rowed had the whole carcass of a cow to dispose of, for which he asked twelve nationals, but came down to ten and a-half, about $6.25.

Next we came to the city of Corrientes, which is large and of a good deal of importance, being the chief northern city of the Argentine.   Here it was that Francisco Solano Lopez made the start with his Paraguayan troops to cross Argentine territory in order to reach his enemies, the Brazilians, which act opened hostilities in what was to be a five years' war, and gave the Argentines a chance to join the Brazilians in the attempt to partition Paraguay among them.   During the war this city was headquarters for the allied armies and fleets.   By this time we were far enough north to have the landscape quite tropical; orange groves were to be seen from Bella Vista up, and their glossy green foliage was lovely against the gray and white adobe walls of the houses and churches of Corrientes.

After the usual official fuss and feathers we went ashore, and I was charmed with the quaint old houses.   The streets are narrow and numerous.   Walking out one day we came to the market, finding, as it was late in the afternoon, only a few women guarding, among other things, piles of oranges, which · sold, to foolish strangers, for fifty cents a hundred.   Quantities of cigars made from native tobacco were there : some of the women were rolling them then against the next day's sales. The tobacco was light in color, but looked good.   These women also make a lace like that of Cordoba, the mesh square and knotted, the pattern tied or woven in.   There were plenty of the familiar peanut, but raw, and we passed them by to enjoy the antics and chatter of two parrots, who were swinging in a ring and having a most jolly time, to judge by the frequent peals of laughter that interlarded their gossip. We stopped at a bank to buy some paper money and became quite intimate with the cashier, while all the clerks came and stood around, gazing with undisguised curiosity; it made one feel like a monkey and a hand organ. However, we heard the family history of the friendly official, and he offered to take us about in his carriage at any time. He said the town was three hundred years old, and it doubtless is. Many of the oldest houses were long and unusually low with tiny windows and small, heavily-barred doorways, a porch along the front, its roof supported at the eaves by black palm-tree trunks, and the roof covered with other varieties of palm trunks that had been slit and scooped out in the center, like a Dutch tile. On the fronts of some of them were bullet marks, souvenirs of revolutions.

There were frequent, heavy showers every day of our stay and the streets a mass of mud, but the raised sidewalks were passable and the crossings fair. Stores were quite numerous, and very good for the situation of the city. Country wagons —prairie schooners—drawn by long lines of oxen were frequently seen, and, as to reach the leaders, a goad with a very long handle was needed, it was often suspended by a rope just under the roof of the wagon, and the driver by reaching up could direct it to the flanks of the oxen without much trouble.

Some of the goads were ornamented with tufts of ostrich feathers. The grand plaza was quite pretty with a monument in the center and a fine municipal building at one corner, shining in its coat of new stucco and paint. Another side of the square is decorated with a mediæval castle-like structure, which is the Cabildo, built in 1816.

Near this latter was the rough brick church of Our Lady of Mercy, and we were much disappointed to find all the doors locked. An arch in a side-wall led into a grass-grown quadrangle with cloisters around it, and we were debating about entering when across the green turf, cantering toward us, came a black horse with rough, long coat. Astride him, his legs sticking straight out, cassock rolled up, and tucked into the rope girdle, was a priest. His shovel-hat well on the back of his head showed a face of pure Guarani type. When he saw us he smiled pleasantly, reined in his charger, and halting, showed us where a rope and bell hung near by. We rang and then he rang, but the porter was probably stowed away in some cell enjoying a siesta, and tying his horse to a post the priest slipped out of the saddle and offered himself as guide after furnishing my husband with a native cigar like the one he himself was consuming. He told us there were 4,000 inhabitants and that the people were very religious ; he was proud of being a native, born twenty-five leagues away, and spoke some Guarani for us, thinking it very odd that we did not speak it. It seems a language of guttural exclamations, and in time we acquired a little of it, but it must be quite a language, for it was the predominant speech of Eastern and Southern South America, as Quichua was of the northern and western parts.

The church was clean and had several altars in good order, but nothing to interest us as much as our guide, who cross-questioned us as to our religious beliefs as well as our country, and finally left us with a blessing and a cheery good-day, trotting off to make a visit in the country.

The church of San Francisco—in another part of the town—has a most imposing look, approached as it is by two colonnades that sweep up to the front in fine curves, but the interior, while large, was a disappointment, barring some old carved-leather coverings to some antique chairs. The paths in the Plaza San Martin were under water, but from the surrounding sidewalk we saw a military figure, with tall shako on head and sword in hand, on foot charging an imaginary foe. The gardens were full of lovely flowers, and it was only necessary to stop and admire to have one's hands filled with the fragrant blossoms of rose and jessamine bushes.

XXVIII.

THE CITY OF ASUNCION—ELEVEN HUNDRED MILES UP THE PARANA AND PARAGUAY.

PARAGUAY'S LONG AND BLOODY STRUGGLE FOR INDEPEND-
ENCE—HER THREE GREAT DICTATORS—INTERVIEW WITH
THE SON OF FRANCISCO SOLANO LOPEZ.

WHEN the town of Corrientes faded from our sight I gazed
up stream with increasing ardor and impatience, for we were
nearing the goal of my desire—the land of dictators and of
a war whose history reads like a grand, bloody romance in
five volumes, one for each year in which the little land-
bound republic of Paraguay held at bay its proud and
powerful neighbors, its people copiously watering the soil
of their native land with their blood in order to preserve
their autonomy and their rights. What matters it that they
fought under and at the command of a tyrant? What if
Francisco Solano Lopez was unnecessarily unjust? and all
the braver their fight if there were brightness neither at

home nor abroad. Think of that little nation fighting for so long Brazil, Argentine, and Uruguay, yet at the end preserving most of its country; and who ever heard of their complaining? Nine-tenths of her people fell, men, women, and children, in battle, of wounds, hunger or disease: the country was untilled; money, jewelry, all, even the most desperate resources for raising money exhausted, yet they took up the burden and began again unknown, unnoticed. One hundred thousand people alone remained in 1870; but their country is wonderfully rich in gifts of nature. The mountains and plains are covered with valuable forests; many streams water it; the climate is tropical, and cultivation of the soil easy. So when the people increase once more and develop their natural riches there seems no reason why they should not take a prominent place in the sisterhood of republics.

Dr. Francia Carlos Antonio Lopez, and after him his son, Francisco Solano Lopez, each in his turn from 1811 to 1870, held Paraguay in their relentless grasp, dictators and tyrants by all we can read and hear—the last seeming the worst of all; yet there is truth in what his son Enrique said to me in Buenos Ayres, when I asked him to tell me of a book which should give a history of the war from the Paraguayan side. "There is none," said he. "Our side has never been written." This same Enrique is a quiet,

self-possessed man, having a lovely home, devoted to his wife
and children—the former, an American by birth, and beautiful. He has a fine library, and kindly loaned me books
upon his native land in all the languages I knew. There
was here a fine picture of his father, in uniform, mounted
on a white horse; not a fine figure—too stout, and the face
Guarani; that is a round Indian face, prominent features,
but the face round. The photograph of his mother, Madame
Lynch, was beautiful. She would have passed for a twin
sister of the Empress Eugenie. He himself looked like a
Spaniard, while the next younger brother, Carlos, was more
blonde and taller, but he lacked the dignity and polish of
Enrique, who is a fine linguist and most kindly satisfied
my curiosity by showing many relics of his father, such as
his field-marshal's baton of blue velvet studded with gold
stars and the ends of the same metal beautifully worked;
a gold riding-whip presented by General Mitre upon the
occasion of a conference; official papers signed by Francia
and all of his successors in office until the war began;
military decorations; a file of a paper in Guarani, which was
published in his father's camp during the whole war, and
many other most interesting things.

Above Corrientes we passed several boats loaded with
oranges, for it was the first of May and the crop was beginning
to come down. They are piled in as we would pile in stones,

filling the whole boat, and that they may hold still more, the sides are built up with a rough basket-work, and the golden fruit put in until it almost overflows. We entered the mouth of the Paraguay River quite late in the afternoon, and our first glimpse of the country was of a low point of land between the Parana and Paraguay, which proved to be an island where 6,000 Brazilians were buried during the war, having died of wounds and disease. It seemed odd, after our hundreds of miles of river traveling, to finally be where we could see both banks, but it was very pleasant—we felt as if we were seeing more. The next morning we passed Humaita, our first Paraguayan town, which was spread out some distance along a low bluff, at which lay two vessels being loaded by women with oranges. The town seemed to have about 1,000 inhabitants, and over a long, low building floated the Paraguayan flag, which consists of three broad horizontal stripes of red, white, and blue, the center one of white bearing mid-way the arms of the country, a lion guarding a pole on which is a liberty-cap. The town was dominated by the ruins of a church which was battered down by the Brazilians. All the houses have thatched roofs. There was no sign of fort or fortification, but a battle was fought there, and a chain stretched across the river to impede the enemy's fleet.

We passed a rather flourishing colony on the Argentine side, and then came to the town of Villa Pilar, of the same size and general appearance as Humaita. A steamer the size of ours was an unusual sight, and when we passed, many of the people came to the bank to see, which pleased us, as we wanted to see them. They were generally dressed in white cotton-cloth, had copper-colored skins, and the women largely predominated. The trees in the woods were lovely, so fresh and green, and there were many flowers. After the mouth of the Vermejo River was passed, the water was clear, which looked so pretty, after the yellow, rushing flood of the Parana. There were crocodiles sunning themselves on bits of beach or stranded logs, and we saw a cross erected to mark the last resting-place of some lonely pilgrim.

The next day we passed several colonies on the Argentine side. That of Formosa is large, and has a *cana* factory, with fields of sugar-cane about it, a fine office for the port officials, and barracks for soldiers. Opposite is a straggling Paraguayan town, built to prevent smuggling. Wherever there was an open space the ground was dotted with palm trees, and banana plants surrounded each house. The next day we began to see hills and wooded mountains in the distance, while along the river the bluffs grew higher and more picturesque. How lovely the tropical scenery looked! The richness of color, the abundance, all such a treat to the eye, while the hills and the mountains seemed so glorious after more than a year of dull, colorless stretches of pampas, that I began to love the beautiful land my-

self, and felt a personal sympathy for the patriotic Paraguayans. It must be so easy to adore such a beautiful land. We
passed the town of Villeta, which is the center of the orange
trade, and near the back was a large shed, underneath which
were piles of oranges, and oxcarts full of them were being
dumped, adding to the accumulation. The peak of Lambare
near the bank, is a curiously shaped affair, which is named for
an Indian chief; its shape conical and so small the base that
it looks as if some one had pared it down. Just beyond we
rounded a point, and there spread before us, following the curving shore, lay the object of our pilgrimage up 1,100 miles of
river, and it seemed hardly true that we had reached Asuncion.
There is a line of wooded hills sweeping around in a grand
curve behind the buildings, and as the ground of the site is
uneven, some buildings stand out very prominently; especially
so does the palace of Lopez, which he began building, its square
tower with four minarets towering over all other buildings, and
vying with the church steeples.

XXIX.

THE PLACE OF LOPEZ.

THE BUSY WOMEN OF PARAGUAY—THEIR REMARKABLE SKILL IN LACE WORK—INDIAN POTTERY AND OTHER CURIOUS WARES—THE MARKETS AND THEIR MANY ATTRACTIONS.

THERE are about 25,000 inhabitants in Asuncion, and we found several good wharves, back of one of which they are building a custom-house that promises to be quite a fine one. Steamers run up twice a week from Buenos Ayres to this city, and when one was in I liked to frequent the wharves to see the bales of mate and tobacco, boxes of cigars, ferns, palms, orchids, and other living plants; parrots, parroquets, small birds, deer, monkeys, and many small animals that were always brought down to be shipped to the lower river ports. There are two street railways, and between their tracks the ground is paved ; otherwise and elsewhere the streets are full of sand, which gets into one's shoes and seems unpleasant, but I heard several people complaining that it was proposed to pave the streets,

15

which they thought would make the city unhealthy, as all of those impurities which now sank into the sand would rest on top of a pavement and poison the air!

Walking along one of the streets, near the river, we came to Lopez's palace, which he had to abandon in an unfinished state and fly before the allies to the northward, retreating until he met death on the banks of the Aquidiban River, not far from the Bolivian frontier. The government is now finishing the building for its own use and it will be a very fine affair. The ground floor and that above are spacious and roomy, with a grand staircase, while a view from the tower takes in the city and surrounding country for miles in every direction. On the city side it has a large grass plat in front and toward the river two very high terraces reach to the bank and command a lovely view of the winding river with its banks. Below ground—in the basement—were numbers of tiny cells for prisoners, some without even a ray of light, and one which was only to be reached by a passage about six feet long, four feet from the ground, and just large enough to shove a man's body through; it gave one the horrors just to look at these places.

Out once more in the soft, balmy air, we found on a street leading to the river and just beyond the palace, a shop where liquid groceries were dispensed and probably exchanged with the ignoble red man for the numerous articles made by him, that were always there on sale. Bows and arrows, earthenware, and carved gourds predominated; the bows and arrows generally have been much used, the bow of wood with rawhide string, and very difficult to bend; arrows of varying length, tipped with wood or spear-shaped heads of iron ground to an edge on both sides.

Most of the pottery was coarse and red, but there were a few fine pieces, among which I secured a large, round bowl, with straight sides, about two feet in diameter, the inside brown, with indistinct patterns in black on it, the outside black, with an all-over Greek pattern in red bands, with white edges to them. There were numbers of grotesque figures of no apparent use, such as horses with lion's mane and tail, dogs with monkeys on their backs, cows with asses' ears and no horns or tail, women with short, fat legs, no feet, and long, slim arms, with a wreath of flowers or a round hat and feathers on the head. These were in red, black, or white, or of all three colors mixed.

The gourds are of all sizes and shapes, small ones for pepper, salt, and other small articles, larger ones for meal and grain, and all prettily decorated, ornamented first with a pattern scratched on with a fish bone or pointed instrument and then colored with different clays. These patterns are always pretty and sometimes beautiful; are always geometrical and never seek to copy the flowing lines of flower, fruit, or other natural objects. In the sandy streets one often met the wild Indian woman with a child or two, trying to sell a few gourds or feather dusters. I bought two gourds of a woman who was so repulsive in face, form, and dirt that it seemed unnatural to see her fondle the baby she carried.

The native Paraguayans are tall and bronze skinned. The women are generally clad in white cotton skirt and manta, and the folds falling in straight lines and draping them from head to foot were very picturesque, and the burden carried balanced on the head gave them erect carriage and even gait. When we met a woman with a bundle that looked like cloth on her head we would say *Nanduti* in a questioning tone, and then, if she had any, the bundle would be lifted from her head and placed anywhere in the sandy street, and we all would sit down to enjoy a trade.

Nanduti is Guarani for spider's-web, and is used to specify a lace as fine as any made in Europe and more charming because of its novelty. It is made with a threaded needle, web and pattern being woven at the same time, and is generally made in wheels, hence the name, and these wheels are put together to form borders for handkerchiefs, fans, yokes for chemises, trimming by the yard, and a coarse variety for sofa pillows, bed covers, and towel ends. The thread used for fine pieces is about No. 300. The workwoman stretches a bit of muslin on a hand frame, threads a needle, and weaves her spider-web wheel, attaching it at the edges to the muslin. When finished, she cuts it loose and begins another. It is very cheap, as one

HANDKERCHIEF, PARAGUAYAN LACE.

can buy for $10 a handkerchief that has taken two months' labor to complete. They prefer gold in payment, as they use it to make puzzle rings and ornaments, and offering it always caused a reduction. It is said that they were taught by the Jesuit mission fathers some 300 years ago, which may be so, but it seems more likely to me that a native manufacture was improved and fostered by the fathers. In these bundles we also found table cloths and napkins of loosely-woven cotton, with bands of insertion down the center and large wheels of *nanduti* set in the corners.

Then there was a coarser knit lace, which is made of unbleached cotton threads and wears like iron; it comes in chemise yokes, edging, and inserting. There would be yokes of darned and embroidered tulle that were gems in their way, and at the bottom of the bundle would be pretty, serviceable hammocks of white cotton or striped twine and with a fringe falling along each side. When the bargain for lace or dry-goods was concluded, to touch our rings would suffice to make the vender bring from her pocket a handkerchief on which would be strung a number of gold puzzle rings made of slender chased rings, eight or nine of them, twisted so to form a solid ring when on the finger and falling apart as soon as taken off, requiring patience and dexterity to replace them. These women make the articles in their own homes all over the country and carry them to the towns for sale, but never sell to stores. If

ever their fine *nanduti* becomes known in this country it is sure
to become popular and take a permanent place among their
finest goods on the counters of our lace merchants.

The market was a perpetual source of delight, and I went
there every day of our stay. Raised two and three steps from
the street was the tall, square building, occupying a square,
and surrounded by a double row of columns reaching to the
roof, the whole colored a deep, dark red. Crouched among the
columns were groups of women and children, their bronze skins
showing plainly each outline where the pure white garments
parted, jet black hair falling down their backs in two braids or
caught up into a careless cluster by a big comb with gold top.

These gold combs were much prized formerly, and the
women divided into two classes, those who had gold combs and
those who had not. These groups were guarding piles of
yellow maize, yams, potatoes, and mandioca. Coming and
going were numbers of white-robed figures bearing burdens on
their heads, from tiny bundles to big red earthen jars filled with
water. Inside was a large, square, open court filled with low
tables covered with merchandise, and all, even those where
meat was cut up, served by women, for the war took so many
of the men that women do all the work and fill all sorts of un-
accustomed places ; a male child being a treasure beyond price
in their eyes, the little naked fellows bare faced around as you
pass that you may notice the sex and envy the mother accord-

ingly. Here we found meat, vegetables, monkeys and other pets, breads of all kinds, and among them a crescent-shaped roll of bread and cheese baked together; lace of the different kinds and native-made jewelry stands, where we purchased gold beads, combs, and ear-rings. There were piles of native cigars —excellent tobacco they are made of—and every one smokes. The best brand is Papa Lucas and they cost \$2 a hundred. Just back of the market is a large barren plaza, where one of the Presidents was once assassinated.

XXX.

THE ANNIVERSARY OF THE INDEPENDENCE OF PARAGUAY.

A BALL AT THE "CLUB FAMILIAR" IN HONOR OF THE OCCASION—THE BELLE OF THE EVENING—NOTABLE PERSONS PRESENT—OLD PALACE OF LOPEZ.

THE present government building of Asuncion is just beyond the unfinished palace of Lopez, on the river bank. It stands apart, surrounded by grass, and is rather an old-looking, two-storied affair. We first saw it on the 14th of May, which is a Paraguayan Independence Day. All the windows were open and the people passing in and out, and two bands playing outside gave the whole a properly festive air, properly festive because President Escobar was holding a reception within. Many military personages were coming and going, and some civilians in broadcloth, but none of the people, none of the masses. They failed to take any interest except in the music, which was continuous, for as soon as one band stopped to take breath the other one piped up. Near-by was a goodly monument, on which we read, " Foundation of Paraguay, 15th of August, 1536. First shout of liberty, 14th of May, 1811. Oath of the Constitution, 25th of November, 1870. Independence Day, 25th of December, 1842." Just beyond was a stretch of green turf in front of the cathedral, which is a fine, large old structure with roomy interior, two of the windows being of stained glass. The high altar is covered with plates of silver, and many ornaments of the same precious metals were about it. There was a curious bit of old sculptured marble for a holy-water basin that we were told came from ancient Rome; if so, it probably has a history, and anyway I longed to hear it speak, that what it had witnessed of the unwritten history of Paraguay might have been poured into our longing ear.

The night of the 14th we were invited to a ball given by the Club Familiar to celebrate the day, and I was all the more anxious to go as it was whispered in the air that the adherents of the political party named " Blue," or Conservative, had agreed to assassinate the ex-secretary of state, Senor Cavallero, that evening at this same ball. He belonged to the Radicals, or " Reds," and it was determined to strike at him because he was believed to be a modern Warwick, the true power behind the throne. As we approached the scene of festivities we noticed double guards at every corner, and at the entrance a file of soldiers was seated, with another file concealed behind a screen of trees in the patio. Either precautions were too well taken or they were ashamed to have a scrimmage before so many naval officers of the mother Republic, whose Stars and Stripes were floating from a war-ship in their harbor for the first time for over thirty years. Anyway the evening passed off quietly, and but for the guards and the absence of some Paraguayan officials and friends, who told me they considered discretion the better part of valor, one might have fancied all at peace.

The club-house is large and the patio was beautifully decorated with flowers, and amidst them was set the supper table and the bands of music placed. Eight connecting rooms were opened for dancing, brilliantly lighted with gas, and as the music was continuous, the floor was always occupied by dancers. As usual, the girls were pretty and the men carried themselves well. Of course there was a sprinkling of Englishmen—one sees them everywhere in this world, struggling for a living, because their little island is full to overflowing, and those who drop over the edges must go somewhere. I was amused to see some of them ostentatiously displaying red or blue handkerchiefs to indicate their political preferences, as if an Englishman born in Britain was ever anything else but an Englishman, or could take any but the most evanescent interest in foreign politics. It takes an Irishman to go heart and soul into another man's fight, and generously spend his blood in a brother's cause. The wife of our vice-consul, Mme. Saquier, bore off the palm for beauty, and as a girl she was called the Flower of Paraguay. Still young, she is beautiful in feature, form, and expression, as well as graceful in movement. Her father was called from his house and shot by order of Francisco Solano Lopez, because he was of Spanish birth, and no foreigner could then live in Paraguay. President Escobar received us with words of cordial greeting and a pleasant smile. He is quite tall, broad-shouldered, with thin brown hair and beard, the latter almost hiding his bad teeth, while his features and skin indicate a certain amount of Indian blood. Afterward we frequently met him riding through the streets, attended by a single orderly. Near him, at the ball, stood Señor Cavallero, a tall, portly, gray-haired man, with an intelligent face. I often wonder if his enemies have killed him yet. Supper was served all the evening, and consisted of croquettes, sandwiches, cakes, port wine, and beer. Quadrilles, waltzes, polkas, and the danza were the dances. The minister of foreign affairs, Señor Centurion, and his wife, were among those we met, his face being remarkable for a bad scar on each side of the jaws, as if a bullet had plowed its way through, and his wife afterward told me that such was the case, and that he received the wound at the time Lopez was killed on the banks of the Aquidiban, her husband having been with him at the time, and escaping by hiding in the woods and remaining there in spite of his terrible wound until the Brazilians had passed on.

The old palace of Lopez, where he resided, is now the post-office, and quite near it is an unfinished copy of the Invalides in Paris, which he intended for his mausoleum. An unfinished theater or opera-house also bears testimony to his passion in the way of erecting large buildings, nearly all of which are unfinished. The outer walls of the theater, rising two stories high, are all that remains of that building, which was so large that it is a wonder as to where he expected to find an audience. I was told that any one who would build or finish off rooms or shops inside the walls could get their rent free for ten years, the government hoping thus to get a finished building, good for some use at the end of a decade. The railway station is a large one, whence starts a line, the first built in South America, for the town of Encarnacion, on the Parana River. It is finished as far as Paraguari, and will soon be extended to Villa Rica. At Encarnacion it expects to meet an Argentine line. We were anxious to make the trip as far as Paraguari, but advised not to, for our time was limited, and we were told that the roadbed had not been repaired since the English originally laid the line, away back in the sixties.

XXXI.

SUBURBS OF ASUNCION.

BRIGHT AMERICAN SCHOOLMA'AMS IN THE PUBLIC SCHOOLS
—HOW MATE LEAVES ARE GATHERED AND PACKED—
PARAGUAYAN MAN-OF-WAR "PIRAPO."

THE pleasantest excursion that we made in the environs of Asuncion was to the country house of Dr. Stewart, the British consul, but a man who has made Paraguay so long his home that he is quite identified with it, and during the war was Lopez's chief medical officer. We rode a long way in the street-car, and finally alighted at the entrance to a shady lane, down which our way lay for some time until we came to a large gate, that gave entrance to a broad, uneven lawn, dotted with trees and sheep, lying in front of a large house, to the left of which were meadows with lovely trees, while to the right the forest stretched a mile in a seemingly unbroken line to the river; the forest belonging to the estate.

Mrs. Stewart and her daughters welcomed us. She is a full-blooded Paraguayan, with skin as white as a Saxon, tall, fine figure, and fine features. She was at home during all the war, and could a tale of hardship and horror unfold did she choose to speak, as her husband's good fortune in escaping after Lopez had doomed him, irritated the tyrant, and he made her suffer accordingly.

Back of the house is a charming garden filled with many strange native fruits and flowers, among them orchids, delicious of odor and fascinating in color and shape. One spike of lavender, of butterfly-like blossoms, with rich, heavy fragrance, lingers especially in my memory. Then there were many strangers that the doctor had sent for, among them a sandalwood tree, tall and flourishing.

Another suburb which is rapidly growing to be a town is called Villa Morra. It is reached by street-cars, and on the way we passed the central cemetery, where I wished to alight and examine; but such a clamor was raised about contracting dreadful diseases that I was fain to be content with a passing glimpse of white head-stones and crosses, decorated with wreaths of artificial flowers and ribbons. Villa Morra was started by an Italian gentleman, who owned the land, and as he also owned a street-car line, he connected the two, built a hotel, laid out villa sites in the forest, and named the place for himself.

We had a nice breakfast at the hotel, which had only a few

bedrooms, but the combination dining and billiard room was unusually spacious. Across the road, in the forest, surrounded by fern-trees and begonias, was a public bathhouse ; the large tubs filled with fresh spring water, looking very cool and inviting. We took tea with some English acquaintances in one of the houses that bordered the road. One of the doors to the parlor opened on to the road, the other into the forest, a place where the ducks and hens met with all sorts of adventures and seldom came home at night as numerous a flock as started out in the morning. The stable was a square of logs piled up to keep the horses from wild animals, and was rather primitive, but all the climate called for.

It was delightful to sit almost surrounded by the forest and watch the shades of green shift and change as the wind passed over the ferns and through the branches of the trees, but the talk of our host and hostess was all of the halcyon days to come, when their ship should have reached port and they be settled once more in England to enjoy life. In the forest were begonia blossoms, and along the roads hibiscus, while the gardens were ablaze with blossoms, a feast of color, and a woman near the Church of San Roque, whom we went to see making ñanduti, gave me some of the largest, finest-colored La France roses that I ever saw anywhere.

The hotel in the city is on the Calle Palmas, and is a large building with nice airy rooms, but none of the modern conveniences. The dining-room is the patio and the food excellent, as well as the fruit. Not far away was the public school, as Paraguay has copied the Argentine in adopting our public school system, and has imported two United States young women to begin the work—a Miss Wales and a Miss Reid. They were furnished with a fine large house, were accumulating excellent apparatus, and were paid good salaries regularly. Of course, it was exile, but Miss Wales seemed too much interested to mind, and Miss Reid was looking forward to matrimony. The children were of the best families and attendance good, the hours of attendance being somewhat longer than with us, and a few extra branches taught.

There were a good many pretty leopard skins for sale, as the animals were numerous farther up country, and a stuffed skin was presented to us, which not only proved a thing of beauty and a joy forever, but kept the mischievous monkey out of the cabin. He first saw it when coming down by way of the hanging lamp, and could hardly believe his eyes; but when he was sure, fled with a howl of terror that brought all hands to the scene. One day, in wandering about, we found an old woman who spoke Spanish, and she invited us into her little hut of two rooms and offered milk to refresh us. Everything was neat as a pin, and in the adjoining room her pretty daughter was teaching a few little fellows their A B C's for a few cents a week each one. Doors and windows habitually stood open, and the passer-by could see plainly what was going on within, and I was struck with the cleanliness and tidiness of the poor people.

Of course, as our visit was in winter, we missed the intense tropical heat and the clouds of insects that annoy one continually by day and by night, but the people were most kind and courteous, opening their houses and entertaining us in every way. Our consul was a bachelor living at the hotel, but he and the vice-consul, Señor Saguier, gave a ball to the officers at Señor Saguier's house, and other festivities were planned, when all were ended by orders for the ship to leave for Buenos Ayres. We used to see great piles of maté bags, and not far from where we were began the *yerbales*, or plains, where the maté tree flourishes. As I have said before, it is a species of holly. *Ilex Paraguayensis* is the technical name, and the leaves are gathered from the wild trees. It does not seem to be cultivated at all.

A fire is built on the ground, over this a dome of brush is built, and this dome thickly covered with maté twigs bearing leaves. When the leaves are dried by the fire they are packed into hide bags, which hide, being raw, is flexible and the maté is forced in with sticks until it is packed as tightly as possible; then the bag is put in the sun to dry and shrink, the result being a package as hard as a stone and very heavy for its bulk. Some packages must have been three feet square at the sewed edges,

16

and others not more than a foot, yet some of the latter would weigh eight pounds. The hair of the animal is left on, which gives variety in color and makes piles of them picturesque.

There was a brick factory and kiln below the city, and here, as everywhere on the river, the houses were made of these kiln-dried bricks and covered inside and out with adobe-like plaster. They have one little-man-of-war, the Pirapo, a small steamer which came down the river while we were there, and when visited by one of our officers he was asked to excuse the appearance of the deck, as they had been in a fight and had not had time to clean up. They then had on board the body of a general who had been killed in the revolution up at San Pedro a few days previously, and as he was quite a man he had a large funeral, the President in person attending.

A few days later we steamed down the swiftly-flowing river and Paraguay vanished from our view to become a memory of green hills; lovely valleys; romantic, heroic history, and pleasant, gracious people. A gem of a country set in the bosom of the South American Continent.

 **BOOKS**

From the Press of the Arena Publishing Company.

Along Shore with a Man of War.

By MARGUERITE DICKINS. A delightful story of travel, delightfully told, handsomely illustrated, and beautifully bound. Price, postpaid, $1.50.

Evolution.

Popular lectures by leading thinkers, delivered before the Brooklyn Ethical Association. This work is of inestimable value to the general reader who is interested in Evolution as applied to religious, scientific, and social themes. It is the joint work of a number of the foremost thinkers in America to-day. One volume, handsome cloth, illustrated, complete index. 408 pp. Price, postpaid, $2.00.

Sociology.

Popular lectures by eminent thinkers, delivered before the Brooklyn Ethical Association. This work is a companion volume to "Evolution," and presents the best thought of representative thinkers on social evolution. One volume, handsome cloth, with diagram and complete index. 412 pp. Price, postpaid, $2.00.

For sale by all booksellers. Sent postpaid upon receipt of the price.

Arena Publishing Company,

Copley Square,   BOSTON, MASS.

BOOKS

From the Press of the Arena Publishing Company.

Songs.

By NEITH BOYCE. Illustrated with original drawings by ETHELWYN WELLS CONREY. A beautiful gift book. Bound in white and gold. Price, postpaid, $1.25.

The Finished Creation, and Other Poems.

By BENJAMIN HATHAWAY, author of "The League of the Iroquois," "Art Life," and other Poems. Handsomely bound in white parchment vellum, stamped in silver. Price, postpaid, $1.25.

Wit and Humor of the Bible.

By Rev. MARION D. SHUTTER, D.D. A brilliant and reverent treatise. Published only in cloth. Price, postpaid, $1.50.

Son of Man; or, Sequel to Evolution.

By CELESTIA ROOT LANG. Published only in cloth.

> This work, in many respects, very remarkably discusses the next step in the Evolution of Man. It is in perfect touch with advanced Christian Evolutionary thought, but takes a step beyond the present position of Religion Leaders.

Price, postpaid, $1.25.

For sale by all booksellers. Sent postpaid upon receipt of the price.

Arena Publishing Company,

Copley Square,   BOSTON, MASS.

www.ingramcontent.com/pod-product-compliance
Lightning Source LLC
Chambersburg PA
CBHW020348030726
47496CB00007B/2051